### JESTER VETERINARY CLINIC
#### Dr. Jack Hartman  Dr. Melinda Woods
MAIN STREET ☙ MILLIONAIRE, MONTANA

PET OWNER                          DATE

ADDRESS

$R_x$

To: Mel   Re: Fake Engagement "Facts":

- ☙ **Proposal.** I popped the question at the clinic in January—
  easy to remember, plus we're always at work...together.
- ☙ **Ring.** Forget simple. I would buy you a diamond! I think we
  agreed one-carat marquise cut with half-carat emeralds—
  I never knew you noticed my eyes were green....
- ☙ **WEDDING DATE.** Be vague, be very vague.
- ☙ Recommend outings at The Brimming Cup for leisurely
  lunch, Pop's Movie Theater for lights-out snuggling, and
  Heartbreaker's for slow dancing.
- ☙ And it couldn't hurt to kiss....

REFILL ___ TIMES

THIS PRESCRIPTION WILL BE FILLED GENERIC UNLESS PRESCRIBER NOTES OTHERWISE IN THE BOX BELOW.

Dispense As Written

Harlequin American Romance proudly launches MILLIONAIRE, MONTANA,
where twelve lucky souls have won a multimillion-dollar jackpot.

Dear Reader,

It's that time of the year again. Pink candy hearts and red roses abound as we celebrate that most amorous of holidays, St. Valentine's Day. Revel in this month's offerings as we continue to celebrate Harlequin American Romance's yearlong 20th Anniversary.

Last month we launched our six-book MILLIONAIRE, MONTANA continuity series with the first delightful story about a small Montana town whose residents win a forty-million-dollar lottery jackpot. Now we bring you the second title in the series, *Big-Bucks Bachelor*, by Leah Vale, in which a handsome veterinarian gets more than he bargained for when he asks his plain-Jane partner to become his fake fiancée.

Also in February, Bonnie Gardner brings you *The Sergeant's Secret Son*. In this emotional story, passions flare all over again between former lovers as they work to rebuild their tornado-ravaged hometown, but the heroine is hiding a small secret—their child! Next, Victoria Chancellor delivers a great read with *The Prince's Texas Bride*, the second book in her duo A ROYAL TWIST, where a bachelor prince's night of passion with a beautiful waitress results in a royal heir on the way and a marriage proposal. And a trip to Las Vegas leads to a pretend engagement in Leandra Logan's *Wedding Roulette*.

Enjoy this month's offerings, and be sure to return each and every month to Harlequin American Romance!

Melissa Jeglinski
Associate Senior Editor
Harlequin American Romance

# BIG-BUCKS BACHELOR
## Leah Vale

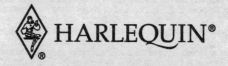

HARLEQUIN®

TORONTO • NEW YORK • LONDON
AMSTERDAM • PARIS • SYDNEY • HAMBURG
STOCKHOLM • ATHENS • TOKYO • MILAN • MADRID
PRAGUE • WARSAW • BUDAPEST • AUCKLAND

Special thanks and acknowledgment are given to
Leah Vale for her contribution to the
MILLIONAIRE, MONTANA series.

For Melissa Jeglinski,
for giving me this wonderful opportunity.

ISBN 0-373-16957-4

BIG-BUCKS BACHELOR

## ABOUT THE AUTHOR

Having never met an unhappy ending she couldn't mentally "fix," Leah Vale believes writing romance novels is the perfect job for her. A Pacific Northwest native with a B.A. in communications from the University of Washington, she lives in Portland, Oregon, with her wonderful husband, two adorable sons and a golden retriever. She is an avid skier, scuba diver and "do-over" golfer. While having the chance to share her "happy endings from scratch" with the world is a dream come true, dinner generally has come premade from the store. Leah would love to hear from her readers, and can be reached at P.O. Box 91337, Portland, OR 97291, or at www.leahvale.com.

## Books by Leah Vale

**HARLEQUIN AMERICAN ROMANCE**
924—THE RICH MAN'S BABY
936—THE RICH GIRL GOES WILD
957—BIG-BUCKS BACHELOR

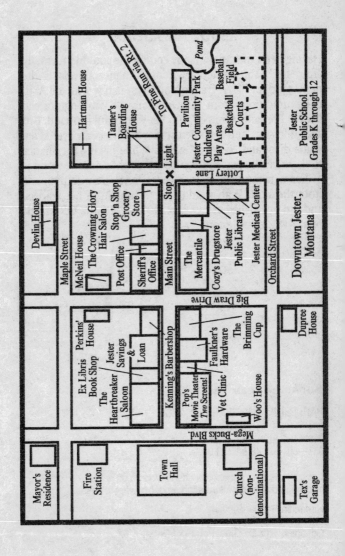

Downtown Jester, Montana

**Mayor's Residence**

**Fire Station**

**Town Hall**

**Church (nondenominational)**

**Tex's Garage**

Mega-Bucks Blvd.

**Ex Libris Book Shop**

**The Heartbreaker Saloon**

**Jester Savings & Loan**

**Perkins' House**

**Kenning's Barbershop**

**Pop's Movie Theater** *Two Screens!*

**Vet Clinic**

**Faulkner's Hardware**

**The Brimming Cup**

**Woo's House**

**Dupree House**

Big Draw Drive

**McNeil House**

**The Crowning Glory Hair Salon**

**Stop 'n Shop Grocery Store**

**Post Office**

**Sheriff's Office**

**Devlin House**

Main Street

**The Mercantile**

**Cozy's Drugstore**

**Jester Public Library**

**Jester Medical Center**

Orchard Street

Stop ✗ Light

Maple Street

**Hartman House**

**Tanner's Boarding House**

To Pine Run via Rt. 2

Lottery Lane

**Pavilion**

**Jester Community Park**

Pond

**Children's Play Area**

**Baseball Field**

**Basketball Courts**

**Jester Public School** Grades K through 12

# *Prologue*

It took everything Jack Hartman had not to end his day by getting kicked in the head. But since he'd already given the Masons' prized Angus cow more help than she appreciated delivering her calf, Jack couldn't blame her.

Preferring his skull intact, he leaned more weight on his hand that held the cow's jerking hind leg still. At the same moment her stomach contracted, he pulled as hard as he dared on the fragile front legs of the stuck calf—all the lathered cow, her musky scent thick in the air, had been able to push out on her own. The muscles in his arms and back strained with the effort, but he didn't quit. Failing to deliver an animal that had the slimmest chance of survival was never an option for this particular vet.

Even if success was bittersweet.

His pull was enough, and the calf's head emerged, followed quickly by the rest of the baby in a wet rush. Steam rose from the calf in the frigid January air let in by the ever-widening gaps between the boards of the Masons' barn walls. Jack let go of the cow's back leg and caught the calf, easing the newborn to the thick straw covering the largest stall in the barn. While Kyle and Olivia Mason might not be able to afford to fix up their old barn, at least they took excellent care of the animals within.

Jack barely had time to clear the calf's nose and mouth to help it pull in its first breath before the baby's mother had turned and taken up her motherly duties of licking and nudging her calf to stand. He straightened and backed away to let the cow's natural instincts do their job.

A hand clapped on his shoulder and he turned to meet Kyle's grin. About twelve years older than Jack's thirty-three years, Kyle Mason was starting to show his age—in the graying of his dark brown hair at the temples, visible beneath his green John Deere baseball cap, and the belly where the beer he used to be able to work off now settled. Kyle and his wife, Olivia, were good people. They'd been there for Jack when he'd needed it, and Jack was glad to be of some help to them.

Kyle squeezed Jack's shoulder before releasing him. "I knew if anyone could save those two, you could."

Jack shrugged and grabbed a towel from the fence to clean his hands off. Until four months ago when he'd finally found some help, he'd been the only veterinarian in the little town of Jester, Montana. And before he'd come eight years ago, they'd had to beg someone to come over from the much larger town of Pine Run, about twenty miles southwest of Jester. But the townsfolk's faith in his abilities warmed him just the same. "She only needed a bit of help." He nodded at the calf. "That little fellow was almost too big for his own good."

Kyle's face lit up. "A bull?"

"A bull," Jack confirmed, using a clean corner of the towel to wipe his too long hair, its light brown darkened by sweat, out of his eyes. He really did need to make time to let Dean Kenning, the town's barber, take a whack at it.

"Hallelujah. Maybe I'll finally be able to afford to fix up some things around here."

Jack followed Kyle's gaze with his own, taking in the boards warped from the extreme southeastern Montana weather and the farm equipment wearing more rust than green paint. But the Masons had held things together better than some folk around here. "I'm sure you'll get a good price for him in Pine Run. Might even be worth the trip to Billings."

Before Kyle could respond, the sound of Kyle's wife of almost twenty years, Olivia, frantically calling for her husband and Jack reached them. "Kyle! Jack! Ky-le! Jaaack!"

While Jack knew that Olivia Mason wasn't given to hysterics—being a teacher in the town's lone school that housed all the kids, grades K-12—one glance at Kyle told Jack something serious must be going on to generate that sort of noise from her. The concern building in Jack's chest was mirrored on Kyle's face.

They had barely left the stall to go see what was

wrong when Olivia barreled through the barn door, letting in a burst of frigid air that lightened the heavy smell of cattle considerably. Her light brown hair flew in her face and the hem of the serviceable blue shirtdress she'd worn to work swirled around her slim form along with the snow that had followed her in. Most telling of all, she hadn't put a coat on.

They rushed toward her.

She was crying. *And* laughing. "Oh, Kyle, sweetheart, you're not going to believe this. And Dean said you, too, Jack. Oh, my word, *all* of us!" She spread her arms, then pulled them back in to cover her mouth. Squealing behind her hands, she started to bounce up and down, looking like a teenager instead of a woman in her early forties.

Kyle grabbed her upper arms to still her and bent to look her in the eye. "Olivia! What is it? What happened?"

She slid her hands from her mouth to her flushed cheeks. "We're rich, Kyle! All of us. We're all *rich!*"

Just as confused as Kyle clearly was, Jack took a step closer to her. "Olivia—"

She stopped him with a wave of her hands, then took a deep breath and straightened, encouraging Kyle to let go of her. Despite her visible effort to calm herself, her voice was still shaky. "Dean Kenning called. The lottery. One of our twelve tickets hit. *We won.* And not just enough for a pizza party, like last time. We won the jackpot. The fifteen of us won the lottery!" She squealed again and launched herself into her husband's arms, nearly knocking his green cap off.

Jack stumbled a step back as if it had been his arms Olivia had jumped into, gripping the towel he still held tightly in his hand. He couldn't believe it.

He had never before played with the loosely defined Main Street Merchants who'd been pooling their money and having Dean drive into Pine Run each week to buy tickets in the Big Draw lottery for the past eight years. As long as Jack had been living in Jester.

But Wyla Thorne had decided not to play anymore, her optimism running as thin as the town's luck, and yesterday morning as Jack was heading into the Brimming Cup for his daily apple Danish, Dean had stepped out of his barbershop to yell across the street at Jack to ask if he wanted to take Wyla's place. For the heck of it, Jack had thrown in a dollar. Talk about it paying off.

Now he had more than enough money to do what he needed to do.

Kyle loosened Olivia's hold around his neck to ask, "How much? How much was the jackpot up to this week?"

Olivia released him and stepped away, her pretty face glowing. "Forty million. We get to split *forty* million."

Kyle whooped and swept his wife up into his arms again, then twirled her around.

Jack's own head was spinning. *Forty million.* "How—" his voice cracked and he had to try again.

"How many ways? Did I hear you say fifteen of us played?"

Kyle stopped so Olivia could answer. "Yes, fifteen total. But married couples only count as one, if they put in only one dollar. Counting Kyle and I, the Perkins, and the Cades as one each, the money will be split twelve ways."

A familiar stab of pain pulsed in Jack's heart at the mention of married couples. He closed his eyes, giving the pain time to settle in to its usual steady ache.

Setting Olivia down, Kyle mumbled to himself and counted on his fingers, obviously doing the math, then said, "After they halve it for taking the lump sum payout, which we did, right?"

Olivia nodded.

"And after taxes, I think that'll leave us all with something like one million, one hundred thousand and change." He moved his mouth as he silently ran over the numbers again, ticking off on his fingers, then waved off his apparent need for accuracy with a frustrated sounding noise. "Anyway, it's definitely well over a million dollars. A million dollars."

He whooped again and whipped off his baseball cap to hit it against his leg. "Damn, Olivia, no more money worries for us!"

Jack absently twisted the towel between his hands as he wandered back toward his stuff.

Over a million dollars.

More than enough to finally get him out of Jester and open a new practice in some other state.

Somewhere far from the memories of all that he had lost here.

The only thing left to do was get his new partner, Melinda Woods, more established, then he could take off.

And maybe, just maybe, make a new start.

He might be able to finally outrun the pain.

# Chapter One

Two months later as Jack sat at his desk, the slight rattle of aluminum blinds against the clinic door brought his gaze down from a pet pharmaceutical company's wall map of where rabies most often occurred in the United States. He'd been fantasizing again about where he'd set up shop next. Through the open door of the clinic's lone office he saw that his partner in the Jester Veterinary Clinic, Melinda Woods, had just burst into the lobby as only a petite, shy woman could, barely rattling the blinds to announce her arrival.

Since she normally didn't make any noise at all when she came in, Jack knew something was wrong. His gut tightened and he frowned. The last thing he wanted was Mel upset. She was the key to his being able to leave Jester.

As she strode toward him, he met her glowering gaze, surprised to find her big brown eyes sparking in a way he'd never seen before. His gut tightened still more. "What's up, Mel?"

"Pigs! That's what. *Pigs.*"

Jack's eyebrows went up. "Pigs?"

She stopped beside the coatrack next to the office door. "Like I don't know from pigs. Me! Of all people!" Yanking her big, tan corduroy jacket off her shoulders, she muttered darkly when the sleeves of her red flannel shirt clung to the jacket's quilted lining. The resulting static electricity had the fine strands of long, blond ringlets that had escaped her ponytail rising in a crazy dance around her head.

She looked more than a little wild around the edges, a far cry from the quiet, efficient woman Jack had grown used to in the six months they'd worked together. It had taken him a long time to find someone willing to work in such a small town so far from anything, and the fact that that someone was as easy to get along with as Melinda was nothing short of a miracle.

Hopefully nothing had happened to change his surprisingly good luck of late.

His confusion and concern mounting, he repeated, *"Pigs?"*

"The Websters' pigs—oh, excuse me," she jerked a hand from her coat sleeve to hold it up in clarification, *"prize-winning hogs."* Her tone dripped a sarcasm he'd never heard from her before. "Mr. Webster won't let me near his *prize-winning hogs.*"

She flung her coat down on the desk that butted against his, fluttering the paperwork he should have been attending to instead of daydreaming about moving. While they were rarely in the office at the same time, there was plenty of space for them both to handle the paperwork the clinic generated, which historically wasn't enough to warrant hiring any office staff.

Though business had certainly picked up since he'd won part of the lottery. Funny how being rich suddenly made a guy popular. Annoyingly popular.

Settling his elbows on the armrests, he sat back in his wooden chair, the swivel mechanism creaking. "Bud Webster wouldn't let you near his hogs? You're kidding."

"Trust me, you have no idea how much I wish I were." She plopped down in her matching chair, which made nary a peep. She, however, let out an exasperated sounding huff and dropped her delicate chin to her chest.

Jack's concern trumped his puzzlement. He'd never seen Melinda like this. From what he could tell, she loved being a vet, and had never once complained about her work, the town or the population of Jester. Just the opposite.

She often spoke highly of the people she was getting to know, even though her shyness made the process slow, and Jack suspected incomplete. He doubted many in town knew just how smart Melinda was. She'd come highly recommended by one of his former professors. What if she changed her mind? What if she decided Jester wasn't the place she wanted to be after all?

A spurt of panic had him leaning toward her. "What exactly happened?"

"Just what I said. Mr. Webster wouldn't let me near his hogs." She lurched to her feet and started pacing the small office, her square-toed work boots clomping heavily on the dark blue vinyl floor. "He said he doesn't want 'no slip of a woman doctoring his hogs.' Slip of a woman," she grumbled, "I'll show him a *slip*."

Jack pulled back his chin. He'd yet to see a critter cross Melinda's path that she couldn't keep a strong, tight hold on, despite being no more than five-four, and she always handled everything with quiet capability. He'd never seen her express herself with so much...passion before.

And despite how threatening her upset was to his intentions to leave, he had to admit the fire in her eyes suited her. But it was a fire that, for Jack's long-term plans, needed to be doused.

"Of all the pigheaded males, that pig farmer has got to be the pigheadedest of them all..." The rest of what she said was lost behind her hands when she reached up and rubbed at her makeupless face as if she were trying to scrub away her frustration.

She dropped her hands and planted them on her jean-clad hips. "He wants you to do the vaccinations."

"Because you're...you're..." he waved a hand at her, struggling to describe her in a way other than the fact that she was outweighed by most large dogs "...not very big?"

She rolled her eyes and threw out a hip. "No. Not because I'm *petite*. Because I'm a woman, Jack. Nothing more than that. Mr. Webster doesn't want a *woman* vet to work on his ranch. And he doesn't care that I grew up on a farm surrounded by pigs, along with just about every other kind of animal.'' The fiery spark in her eyes turned to a watery shimmer and her defiant expression started to crumble slightly. "I know from pigs, Jack." Her voice sounded a little strangled.

His own throat closed up in response. He hated to see a woman cry. It was one of the reasons he'd become a veterinarian instead of a physician. You didn't have to come up with something good to say to make a suffering animal feel better.

Worried by the degree of her aggravation, he rose from his chair and went to her, placing what he hoped would be calming hands on her shoulders. He felt her rigid stance instantly soften and melt. "I know you do, Mel. But the old guard—farmers like Bud Webster—they're still living in a different century. And I don't mean the most recent one. They'll see soon enough that you know what you're doing."

"How? When they won't let me through the gates?"

Her heat seeping into his palms, Jack realized with a jolt that this was the most contact he'd had with a woman in five years and dropped his hands from her slender shoulders. He turned to look at the map on the wall again. At all the places he could go.

The need to leave Jester and the pain that ate away at his insides like a slow-growing cancer flared white-hot. He could have left the day he'd received his lottery check, but he'd wanted to see Melinda securely established in the practice he planned to simply sign over to her so he could leave with no strings attached.

If some of the townspeople refused to accept her, though…

He pulled in a heavy sigh and ran a hand through his hair. It didn't matter. He couldn't stay. Jester held too many memories, too many dreams that would never be realized. Even the dingy statue on the Town Hall lawn of Caroline Peterson, atop her horse, Jester, the town's namesake, brought echoes of laughter and the true story about how the wild horse was really tamed—not with grit and bluster, but patience and sugar.

He turned back to Melinda, absently noticing how her high temper had added an attractive flush to her already sun-kissed cheeks and a golden glow to eyes he had previously only thought of as brown. "Pretty soon they won't have a choice if they want to keep their *prize-winning hogs* healthy."

Her finely arched blond brows came together, then she stilled. "How so?"

"They can't very well refuse to let you treat their livestock if you're the only vet within miles."

JACK'S WORDS hit Melinda like an unexpected blast of frigid, Montana winter air, freezing the breath in her lungs as quickly as fog to glass. While he'd been talking about leaving since the day he'd given her a spot in his practice, she didn't want him to go.

Granted, the prospect of virtually being handed an established veterinary clinic had been the sweetest part of the deal when she'd first signed on, but even without that offer she probably would have agreed to partner with Jack because Jester was exactly the sort of place she wanted to spend her life. She could continue to live in her beloved home state of Montana, be close enough for her mother to afford to call and check up on her like she insisted on doing every Sunday, but still be far enough away from the father Melinda had never been able to please. The one thing she couldn't change about herself was the fact she'd been born a girl.

Then there was Jack, himself.

She'd never forget walking into this office for the first time and nearly being floored by how handsome he was. He'd been sitting with the heels of his brown work boots propped on the corner of the desk, his long, muscular legs stretched out in jeans. The light chambray shirt he'd had on clung to his broad shoulders, and where he'd left it unbuttoned at his neck showed off a sprinkle of chest hair that matched the thick, slightly wavy light brown hair hanging to his collar. His position, along with the set of his square jaw and wide, sensuous mouth, exuded such confidence and animal magnetism it was a wonder she could speak at all.

But unlike her father, and even the guy she'd thought she had a future with in college, Eric Nelson, Jack had wanted to hear what she had to say, so he'd coaxed her past her nervousness and awareness of him enough that she'd landed the partnership despite her relative inexperience. She'd still had to prove herself, though, which was something she had plenty of experience with.

Even on that first day he'd mentioned leaving Jester, that because he'd lost his wife—a loss that had instantly made her ache for him—he should move on, away from Caroline's hometown. But he'd talked so often since then of leaving without ever taking steps to do it that she'd ceased to believe he actually intended to leave. He seemed so ingrained in the town, so a part of its pulse.

She forced herself to pull in a chest-warming breath. "You say that like you mean it."

A muscle in his jaw flexed. "This time I do."

Melinda felt gut punched. She struggled not only to breathe, but to keep the air moving in and out steadily. Today just wasn't her day. She should have stayed in bed with her cats asleep on her feet.

But she'd never been the type to hide from life. To temper her father's disappointment over her being a girl, she'd pulled more than her weight around their farm while growing up, whether he noticed or not. It wasn't her fault she was not only female, but short and quiet. Being the only kid on a farm a long way from most everything, with no one but animals to talk to, didn't make for a sparkling conversationalist.

She couldn't retreat and complain to her critters over this one, though. Simply venting wouldn't make her feel better, wouldn't allow her to accept the outcome, because, bottom line, the outcome was unacceptable to her.

Jack couldn't leave.

She met his gorgeous green gaze, for once blocking from her mind how they exactly matched the sweetest grass in springtime, and dared to ask, "Why now? I sort of figured that when you didn't leave two months ago after picking up your share of the lottery that you'd decided to stay." He was such a part of Jester, she couldn't imagine the town without him.

Just as she couldn't imagine her life without him. She was such a fool, but she couldn't help it. From their very first meeting she'd wanted Jack Hartman. He'd been so kind, dropping his feet from the desk and leaning his elbows on his knees to make his powerful body smaller. He'd coaxed her to talk about herself, about the kind of veterinary practice she wanted to make her life's work.

All he'd wanted was a partner he could leave his practice to.

He shifted his gaze to the wall. "I didn't leave after I got the money because the timing wasn't right then." He went back to the file cabinet and reached up to straighten the framed photo on it, his fingers lingering. It was something he usually did only when he thought no one was looking.

She usually was. He drew her gaze to him like a skittish creature is drawn to a soothing voice. She knew she shouldn't be attracted to him, had heard all about his painful past. Jester was such a small town. Everyone knew everyone else's business. Or at least thought they did.

Thank goodness no one knew how she felt about Jack. She'd already once had to publicly suffer for loving a man who hadn't loved her back, ditching her ugly in front of a crowd of their friends at college when someone better came along. She could never face that sort of humiliation again. Though it was sheer torture, she was much safer loving Jack in secret.

Her romantic sufferings aside, she wouldn't trade for anything the happiness she felt working with him, often going days without actually seeing him if one or the other of them was out on calls. But walking into the office after he'd been there, the faint smell of his no-nonsense aftershave lingering in the air and the wonderful scrawl of his handwriting on notes he'd leave her about where she was needed next never failed to make her smile. The notes were always about work, but their informality always warmed her heart, despite that he almost exclusively used his nickname for her, Mel.

That casual shortening of her name, while undoubtedly unconscious, drove home the fact that he didn't see her as a woman. It was so stupid that the one man to have given her the thing she craved most—respect for what she did—pretty much from the start, was the one man she wanted to notice what she had to offer as a woman. She rubbed a hand over her face again. She really needed to pick a side and stick to it.

Dropping her hand to her lap, she asked, "But the timing is right now?"

Jack cleared his throat in a telling way then said, "I can't stay."

Melinda's heart twisted and ached in her chest. For

the millionth time she wished she could pull him to her and heal him. But all she would probably end up doing would be making a bigger fool of herself. Even if Jack were to notice what she could offer him as a woman, there was a very real chance that what they said about him around town was true—that he'd never get over the death of his wife and their unborn child. How could she compete with the memory of the kind of love she could only dream about?

She couldn't.

Instead of risking embarrassment by trying to comfort him, she asked, "Why now, Jack? Hasn't it been five years since…" she trailed off, unable to put to words what caused him such pain. He'd never spoken to her directly about the car accident. Though she knew from people like Dean Kenning, who thought the world of Jack, that he hadn't been with his wife, five months pregnant, when the accident had happened. A fact that only deepened the wound to Jack's psyche.

Jack finally nodded, running a finger down a clearly familiar course on the dark-wood frame. "It's been five and a half years, actually." He gave a half shrug. "But time isn't going to make any difference. This town holds a lot of painful memories for me, and I don't think one hundred years could make them go away."

Melinda closed her eyes, Jack's pain reverberating inside of her even with the desk separating them. She never could have withstood such a loss. The fact that Jack had weathered such an awful thing without becoming bitter and useless made Melinda love him all the more. Too bad that when it came to love, she simply didn't measure up.

He surprised her by continuing. "Jester was Caroline's town, you see. She was the one who'd grown up here. I'm from Yakima, over in Washington, but my parents have since moved to Florida to be near my older brother and his wife. Caroline and I met at Washington State University." He waved a distracted hand at his framed diplomas on the back wall.

"Even though her family had moved to Coeur d'Alene, Idaho, right before she started high school and are still there, she wanted to come back to Jester. A couple generations back, her family had settled the town." He glanced up at Melinda, the color of his eyes deepened to moss by the memories. "You know that statue on the Town Hall lawn?"

"Of course." She walked or drove past the moldering looking bronze statue of a woman on a bucking horse everyday. She rented a little house just down from it on the other side of the street. One of the first things she'd learned about the town was the legend of how Caroline Peterson—a mere slip of a woman, no less—had broken the seemingly unbreakable stallion, Jester. It was telling that the old geezers back then had named the town after the horse instead of the woman on him.

"Well, that woman is my Caroline's ancestor and namesake. My wife felt she belonged in Jester. She loved the idea of being connected to a place. So after the wedding, we moved here."

"But you don't feel connected to Jester? Even after eight years?"

"It's Caroline's town." He looked back at the framed photo of the pretty brunette with the glowing smile that Melinda hadn't been able to keep from studying when alone in the office. How could a woman not smile that way with a man like Jack in her life? Then to have that life cut so short...the unfairness of it all had made Melinda weep inside.

She crossed her arms over her aching heart and faked a nonchalance she didn't feel. "Where will you go?"

Jack cleared his throat again and visibly pulled himself from his thoughts—probably memories of his beautiful wife and the future they'd planned together—by straightening his strong back and squaring his broad shoulders. "I don't know yet."

"You don't know?"

"No. I haven't decided...exactly...where..." He moved toward the map on the wall.

Relief flooded her, providing just enough hope to bolster her. "So you're not leaving town soon."

"I am."

His simple statement, said with such conviction, slapped her hope down for good.

"I've only stayed this long because I couldn't leave the town without a vet. But then you came. Now I just need to get you established before I leave."

His mention of her being established brought back her anger in a rush, only now it was coupled with the bitter taste of yet another fantasy that would never become reality. "I don't see how that's ever going to happen when some people in town won't let me treat their animals."

"Given no choice, they'll come around."

While she had never disagreed with him in the entire six months she'd known him—never had cause to—Melinda shook her head adamantly. Even if she wasn't crazy about him, she wanted—needed—the farmers to respect her because of her abilities as a vet, not because she'd be the only vet available to them. She needed more time to prove herself. To prove she was as good a vet as any man.

She had to convince Jack to stay longer.

Just as important, she needed to squelch her feelings for him completely so she could concentrate on earning the respect she craved more than anything else. Even more than love.

# Chapter Two

"You can't go, Jack."

Melinda's blurted declaration startled Jack from his musing about where he might move to, where he could go to outrun the past. He'd never seen this sort of assertiveness from her before. Melinda was normally very quiet yet affable.

He'd grown so comfortable with her gentle presence, her reliability, that he occasionally forgot whether she was in the office or out on a call when he was treating a small animal in the examination room.

She was also a damn good vet. She had a way of handling the most difficult of animals, large or small, seemingly reassuring them that she would make whatever pain they might have go away. He had no reason to worry about leaving the animals of Jester in her capable hands.

He'd never seen this side of her, though. He raised his brows at her.

Melinda's cheeks reddened, but her determined stare didn't waver.

Why didn't she want him to go?

His mind drew a blank. He knew she could handle the practice. He tilted his head at her and asked, "Why not?"

Her jaw worked, but her full lips remained sealed and she looked away before he could figure out what emotion her big brown eyes held. Finally, she said, "Because…well, because…" she trailed off and started to fidget.

Alarm swelled in his gut. What if she'd decided she didn't want to stay either?

He opened his mouth to coax her reasons out so he could convince her otherwise but the crash of blinds against the door to the clinic stopped him.

Jack looked over the top of Mel's head in time to see Mary Kay Thompson complete her entrance into the clinic—twice as loudly as Mel had—with a flip of her shoulder-length, permed blond hair, no less, and clutching her obese orange tabby cat, Pumpkin, to her chest.

He would have gaped at Mary Kay's outfit if he hadn't grown so used to her outrageous—and down-right foolish, considering the weather—getups. Today she'd put on open-toe, yellow shoes with low but spiky heels, bright orange-and-yellow flowered tight pants that only reached her sculpted calves—Mary Kay was the only person he knew of around Jester to have her very own stair-climbing machine. Instead of wearing a parka or heavy coat like a sane person, she'd pulled on a vinyl-looking, unlined, bright yellow slicker. He'd lay money on the guess that she had on a matching tank top beneath the slicker.

The woman routinely risked hypothermia in the name of fashion. Or more likely, in blatant attempts to attract a man. Since his lottery win, Jack had the unfortunate distinction of being that man.

She swiveled toward the office door. "Jack! Thank goodness you're in."

He suppressed a groan. It wasn't that Mary Kay wasn't a nice gal, it was just that she was so… ragingly single. Most eligible men—whom she should have realized by now he wasn't one of—in these parts steered clear of her. Thanks to Pumpkin, a run-of-the-mill barn cat Mary Kay insisted was a rare type of Persian purebred that only he could treat, Jack had no choice but to weather Mary Kay's determination head on.

He cleared his throat. "Actually, Mary Kay, I was just on my way out. But Dr. Woods, here, can take a look at Pumpkin—"

"Now Jack," Mary Kay interrupted. "You know how delicate Pumpkin is."

Jack looked skeptically at the rotund, very robust appearing cat hanging over Mary Kay's arms. The only delicate thing about Pumpkin was the silly pink, rhinestone-studded collar and matching leash Mary Kay put on him. Didn't the woman realize she was living in a very rustic part of Montana?

"I really don't think he can bear the upset of being handled by a stranger. No offense, Melinda." Mary Kay's apology to Mel sounded genuine, despite her absurd reasoning.

It hit him that Mary Kay was yet another Jester resident to snub his partner for a ridiculous reason. He glanced at Mel. She had crossed her arms over her chest, and though she was smiling reassuringly at Mary Kay, her smile looked tight around the edges. Great.

"Please, Jack." Mary Kay reclaimed his attention. "There must be something wrong with Pumpkee. He's been coughing that awful cough again."

The cough the cat had yet to cough in anyone's presence other than Mary Kay's.

And because she lugged the huge thing everywhere with her—probably for warmth—Jack had a hard time believing Pumpkin was anything but fat and spoiled. Still, he was duty-bound to check the cat out.

"All right, Mary Kay. I'll take a quick look at him." Jack gestured toward the clinic's lone examining room.

Mary Kay smiled triumphantly and headed in.

Jack leveled a look at Mel. "I want to finish our discussion. This'll only take a second. Okay?" If needed, he'd go blue in the face convincing her that she could handle the practice on her own.

She shrugged and looked away. He couldn't tell if the fight had gone out of her, or if Mary Kay's ad-

ditional refusal to let Mel treat her animal had been
the straw that broke Mel's spirit. Lord, he hoped not.

The pestering he was getting from Mary Kay and
some of the other ladies in the area, not all of them
single, with supposedly sick animals and a shared fantasy of landing themselves a millionaire, was becoming too much to take. He needed Mel happy so he
could leave. Soon. The constant reminder of his avail-
ability had made the memories of the reasons behind
it that much harder to bear.

"I'll be right back," he assured her.

She waved him off and sat down, her attention on
the paperwork stacked in once neat piles on his desk.

Jack blew out a breath and turned to leave the office. As he walked out he grabbed his seldom-used
white lab coat off the rack next to the door and pulled
it on. As armor went, it was a sorry thing, but as of
late his professionalism was the only defense he had
against women like Mary Kay. The situation wasn't
helped by the fact that after one of the entertainment
news crews that now routinely haunted Jester had followed him out on a call and caught on tape his attempts to calm a bucking horse, he'd been dubbed
The Big-Bucks Bachelor by the press. As if he didn't
have reason enough to get out of town.

He made a point to leave the office door open as
well as the door to the exam room after he went in.
He didn't want to give any sort of impression to anyone.

Mary Kay obviously felt the opposite. Rather than

placing Pumpkin on the exam table, she'd set him on the ground and had hitched one of her hips on the table. She'd managed to strike a pose with the subtlety of an alpha female, with her jacket off her shoulders—he'd been right about the tank top, only it was white, and very thin. She'd catch pneumonia for sure this winter.

She eyed the open door, then surprised him by calling out, "Oh, Melinda, I almost forgot. I noticed on my way in that your truck is parked right under a huge icicle hanging off the clinic's sign. While that truck of yours is already kind of beat-up, you might want to move it before that icicle drops and you end up with a great big dent in your hood."

The sound of Melinda's chair scraping on the vinyl floor reached them, and Jack turned in time to see her leave the office. With her coat dragging behind her and muttering in a very un-Melinda way under her breath, she stomped her way to the front door.

After Melinda left, Jack turned back to Mary Kay. Her smile would have made any feline proud.

"Everyone knows how much she loves that crummy old truck," she said by way of explanation.

It was true. Melinda made no secret about her pride in her truck, willing to take the ribbing doled out to anyone who actually washed a work vehicle on a regular basis in the dead of winter. As a born and bred Montanan, she should know better. Although she'd once mentioned that the truck had been the only thing her father had ever given her. He'd thought there'd been a shadow of pain darkening her brown eyes after she'd said it. She'd had the chance to elaborate, but she hadn't. And he hadn't asked. It wasn't his place to pry.

Flashing a saucy grin, Mary Kay returned her attention to Jack.

He pointedly shifted his attention to Pumpkin, who looked annoyed over having to actually touch the ground. "Okay, big fella, lets have a listen to those lungs." He started to squat down in front of the cat, but Mary Kay grabbed hold of the lapels of his lab coat and hauled him against her.

Surprised and off balance, Jack had no choice but to flatten his hands on the polished metal table and lock his elbows to keep from toppling onto her. The strength of her mercantile-bought perfume made his eyes water.

Apparently oblivious to his distress, in a surprisingly accurate Marilyn Monroe-like breathlessness, Mary Kay said, "Let's stop beating around the bush, Jack, and just do what animals like us are supposed to do."

His gaze went instinctively to the other door out of the exam room, the one that they brought contagious or severely injured small animals through. But she had too good of a hold on him. "Mary Kay, please," Jack demanded. He tried to straighten away from her, but she turned out to be remarkably strong.

"No, I'm the one willing to beg. I'm willing to do anything to be the one tamed by your great, big, strong hands,'' she purred and once again tried to pull him down with her onto the table.

No way was he going to let that happen. But his worn-thin professionalism kept him from physically removing her from his person.

''Don't fight it, Jack. We'd be so good together. Can't you see that? Haven't you felt it building over the years, darling?''

Positive he hadn't exchanged more than the usual pleasantries and professional advice regarding Pumpkin, he adamantly shook his head. ''Really, Mary Kay—''

''Shh.'' She cut off what was going to be a fervent denial by placing the pads of her pink-polished fingertips of one hand over his mouth. ''No. You're right. This isn't the time for words, it's time for action. Let me show you just how lucky you really are, Jack.''

He tried to take a step back, but Pumpkin, undoubtedly looking for revenge against the usurper who'd taken his place on his mistress's lap, had circled Jack's legs and wound the leash that Mary Kay still had looped over her wrist around him. It was all Jack could do to keep from falling backward on his butt or forward onto Mary Kay.

If it came to it, he'd pick hitting vinyl in a heartbeat. He would have never dreamed Mary Kay would become so aggressive in her bid to land a millionaire. Though he shouldn't be surprised. Even the mayor's assistant, Paula Pratt, had suddenly shown up with a pet so she'd have an excuse to come to the clinic. The mayor, after all, hadn't been one of the group he'd dubbed The Main Street Millionaires.

Mary Kay tugged again, her bright blue eyes glinting with determination. "Give me one good reason why not, Jack. Just one," she huskily challenged, leaning yet closer in a clear invitation for a kiss.

Ten compelling reasons instantly came to mind, but none of them were particularly flattering to Mary Kay. While her pursuit of him, obviously fueled by his newfound wealth, was extremely annoying, it didn't earn her his cruelty. But thanks to the effort involved in trying to keep his balance and avoid her puckered lips lined in a shade a heck of a lot darker than her coral lipstick, his brain had a hard time coming up with a nice reason.

The first and foremost truth popped from his mouth. "Because I'm already involved with someone." He always would be.

Mary Kay froze, then frowned. His state of perpetual mourning had never been a secret in Jester, and was the main reason he'd been left alone by the women in town. But over a million in the bank apparently overrode their pity.

The skepticism plain on her meticulously made-up face, she pulled back and challenged, "Who?"

Now he'd stepped in it.

Figuring the rest of that particular truth wouldn't buy him a respite but instead earn him the standard lecture on the benefits of moving on, he mentally scrambled for a name. He couldn't just make a girl-friend up, even one who might live out of town. He was far too visible around Jester, and didn't leave often enough to get a story like that to fly. Besides, in a town of 1,500 people, everyone generally knew everyone else's business.

Just when Mary Kay's frown was turning to exasperation, the clinic's door opened and Melinda returned with a blast of cold air that matched her icy expression. With a glancing glare in their direction that let him know Mary Kay had sent Melinda on an unnecessary trip outside, Melinda stomped back into their office.

It dawned on Jack that the only woman he spent any amount of time with alone was his currently grumpy partner. He could easily be having a relationship with her that no one would know about.

Without further thought he announced, "Mel. I mean, Melinda. I'm currently involved with Melinda." And just in case Mary Kay expected him to be willing to cheat, he threw in, "*Seriously* involved." He took advantage of Mary Kay's shock and extracted himself from her grip.

Looking down, he stepped out of the tangle Pumpkin had made of the leash. He started in on the explanation he was certain she would demand. "Since we work together, we'd prefer to keep it quiet, you understand—" He looked back at Mary Kay, and her expression stopped him.

She was softly saying, "Ah," and nodding her

head as if he'd just pointed out something obvious, like the fact chicken coops stink.

She slipped off the examination table. "Why didn't you say so in the first place, Jack? Sheesh," she muttered as she bent to pick up her rotund cat. "I could have spent all this time hanging at The Heartbreaker Saloon, working on Dev," she groused on her way out of the room.

Jack's brows went up. That had been easy. A little too easy. His luck couldn't be that good. "So you don't want me to take a look at Pumpkin?" he offered while following her into the small waiting area.

"Naa, that's okay." She waved him off as she continued toward the front door. "Pumpkee's tougher than he looks."

Considering that Pumpkee looked like the feline equivalent of a Sumo wrestler, that was saying something.

"Well, if you're sure…" he trailed off, hoping his pleasure over his excuse working wasn't too obvious.

"I'm sure. Catch you later, Jack."

"'Bye, Mary Kay, Pumpkin."

Jack closed the door behind her and whistled low through his teeth. That had been a close one. While lying wasn't his thing, no matter how white the lie, in this instance it had certainly been the lesser of two evils. He doubted he could have convinced Mary Kay that the only woman he would ever want in any way was already gone from his life.

That fate had already decided he would spend his life alone.

Besides, he was leaving Jester.

He turned toward the office, intent on making sure Melinda was on board with his plan, but she was already heading out into the waiting area, her coat on and her vaccination kit in hand.

"Where are you going? I want to finish our discussion."

She stepped around him and made for the door. "Sorry, Jack. But I'm due out at Wyla Thorne's place in fifteen minutes. At least *she* doesn't mind having a woman vaccinate her pigs."

He pulled in a deep breath and followed her. "We'll get everything straightened out, Mel. I promise."

The look she gave him as he held the door open for her said, *yeah, right.*

But he meant it.

He had no choice.

JACK HAD ALL of an hour of peace, having finally forced himself to focus on the paperwork that needed to be done, before the blinds on the door rattled again. He braced himself, wondering which supposedly love-struck lady with a mysteriously ill pet would appear next.

He sent up a silent prayer that it wouldn't be the mayor's curvaceous, blond assistant, Paula Pratt. Her newly acquired, tiny beige Chihuahua, Angel—the dog's original owners had called him Killer—was only happy snuggled up inside the front of the woman's coat, and whenever she drew close to someone, the dog growled. It sounded eerily like her abundant breasts were snarling. And whatever it was that little dog had wrong with him, only a truly gifted animal psychologist could cure.

Jack's prayer was answered when much older and rounder Stella Montgomery came through the door, her platinum-blond curls protected from the weather by a clear plastic rain hat and her peacock blue, heavy winter coat brushing the tops of her sheepskin-lined boots. She caught sight of him in the office and her seemingly permanent smile widened.

He automatically smiled in return. Stella was a real sweetheart. She lived over at Gwen Tanner's boardinghouse, and was forever seeing to everyone's happiness and the health of their love life, where warranted. But she never went there with him.

Not minding the interruption since it was Stella, he pushed his chair back and stood. "Well, hello, Stella." He came around his desk and went to greet her. "How are you today?"

"Oh, I'm marvelous, Jack. Just marvelous." Her pleasantly plump cheeks held more of a rosy glow than usual. And her blue eyes positively twinkled.

"Good. Good."

She smiled at him.

Puzzled, Jack waited, but she didn't explain her

presence. To his knowledge, Stella didn't own any pets.

She simply smiled at him some more.

Rocking back on his heels and burying his hands in the pockets of his lab coat that he'd forgotten to take off, he asked, "So, what can I do for you? Do you need help moving something…?"

"Oh, no. Nothing, really. I just thought I'd stop by and say hello. I noticed Dr. Wood's truck isn't out front. Is she on a call?" She reached up and patted at very curly hair through its protective barrier in a very feminine way.

A sizzling arc of panic went to ground right through the bottoms of his feet. No. Not Stella. She had to be in her mid- to late-fifties.

But she was also single.

Then the reminder of why she was still single cooled him in a rush of relief. She had loved and lost also, though she and her young man hadn't had the chance to marry, their engagement ending tragically with his death. Stella, along with ol' Henry Faulkner who had lost his wife ten years ago, understood why Jack didn't feel the necessity to *move on*.

Still, her obvious delight made him nervous. "Yes. Melinda is out at Wyla's, I believe. Vaccination time. Can I get you some coffee, tea…" He was pretty sure Melinda had heated some water before she left the first time this morning and had a decent selection of instant coffee and tea bags to warm them up after being out treating livestock in the freezing weather.

"You are a dear, but no, thank you." She found an escaped blond curl and tucked it back undercover. "Oh, you know, Irene and I thought we'd do some baking. What sort of cake do you like best, Jack?"

"Cake?"

She smiled even more sweetly and nodded encouragingly.

He shrugged. "Chocolate, I guess."

"Chocolate. Wonderful. With raspberry filling?"

He shrugged again, wondering what his opinion had to do with anything. "That's always good."

"Wonderful, wonderful." Her pleasure was amazing. "Well, I better let you get back to work. Have a wonderful day, Jack." She wiggled her fingers at him and was back out the door before he had a chance to respond.

*Wonderfully* bemused, he stared at the door for a moment, then went back to his desk. That was odd. Especially considering the fact it was Gwen who usually did the baking. She made the most incredible pastries. He made a mental note to stick his nose in at the bookstore across the street, Ex-Libris, where Amanda Bradley let Gwen sell her baked goodies, and snag a muffin or two before he headed home. Perhaps Stella and Irene Caldwell, who also lived at Gwen's boardinghouse, were helping out in the kitchen. That was very likely, since Irene treated Gwen more like a granddaughter than a landlord. He shrugged and went back to work.

Not fifteen minutes passed before Irene blew into

the clinic's waiting room, a cheery yellow scarf tied over her gray hair and a puffy, quilted black coat bundled around her. In her early sixties, Irene had really found a place to belong when she moved into the boardinghouse six years ago. Her husband had passed away four years before that, and without any children of her own, she'd been too alone.

She spied Jack and headed for him before he had time to get up. "Jack, dear! I'm so glad you're in. I have a quick question for you, if I may?"

He set his pen down. Clearly, this was going to be one of those days. "Of course, Irene. What can I do for you?"

"Not a thing. It's only that Stella and I are making a tape of everyone's favorite slow songs for, ah, for the Founder's Day celebration dance, and we were wondering what your favorite is? To dance to? Ah, slow?"

"I thought you and Stella were baking today."

"Are we?"

He raised his brows. Doddering was one thing these older ladies were not.

"Oh, yes." She put a hand to her cheek and laughed. "Of course we are. But we're also making a tape. Of music. To dance slow to."

Jack immediately thought of the song he and Caroline had danced to for the first dance at their wedding. On the sly she'd arranged for the band to start out with a traditional love song, then switch to playing a punk rock song about a white wedding. She'd laughed so hard at the look on his face. If only they could have stayed in that moment. Happy. Safe.

His thoughts must have shown in his expression, because the smile lighting Irene's softly lined face faltered. Not wanting to distress her, he threw out the first song that came to mind.

She smiled in obvious relief. "Ooh, that's a good one, Jack. Thank you, dear." She turned on her sensible heel and hurried out.

The door had barely shut behind her before it opened again. Only this time it wasn't to what he considered a friendly face. Marina Andrews, the blond TV news reporter from a station in Great Falls, along with her cameraman, who'd made Jester their home away from home since the lottery win, came into the waiting room. He could understand their attention right after the win. What had happened *had* been newsworthy. To a point. And certainly for a limited amount of time. In Jack's mind, that time was up. Their continued attempts to dig up a story where there wasn't one anymore was wearing on him.

And that big-bucks bachelor routine definitely hadn't earned them any points.

"Dr. Hartman, might we—"

The phone rang.

Saved by the bell. Jack held up a stilling hand and picked up the receiver with the other. "Jester Veterinary Clinic. Dr. Hartman speaking." He put on the airs for the sake of his audience.

"Jack, it's Ruby Cade."

"Hey, Ru—"

"I need you, Jack. Right now."

For the first time in nearly two months those words coming from a woman didn't illicit dread from him. Not only was Ruby married, she was a fellow lottery winner. Though Jack couldn't recall the last time he'd seen Ruby's husband Sam around town. Since Sam was a military man of some sort, his absence shouldn't be cause for note. But Ruby owned The Mercantile just down Main Street from the clinic with Honor Lassiter and lived in the apartment above the store.

And she didn't have a pet.

He cleared his throat. "Ah, what can I do for—"

She cut him off. "It's that damn goat, Jack. The one that's been hanging around town." Her upset was clear in the quaver of her voice. "It must have wandered into my back storeroom when we were unloading a delivery earlier. Now it's got its head stuck inside a damn bucket and is crashing all over the place. It kicks when we try to get a hold of it. Please, can you come right over and help us before it destroys my stock?"

Ruby never swore, and it was strange to hear her so rattled. But she had been unusually emotional ever since the lottery win.

"I'll be right there, Ruby." Jack hung up, thankful he had an excuse to leave. He grabbed his bag from the floor next to his desk, checking quickly to make sure it contained his heavy-duty clippers. If he recalled, the little billy goat that made occasional forays into town from who-knew-where had horns long enough to keep its head stuck in a bucket.

He stood and went to the coatrack near his office door and pulled his heavy, dark brown canvas barn jacket off the rack. Slipping into it, he met the eyes of the eager reporter. The cameraman's face was already buried behind his camera. "I'm sorry, but I have to go."

"Can you just answer a couple of quick—"

He held up a hand again. "It's an emergency. Sorry."

Marina's face glowed, clearly having picked up the scent of opportunity. "We'll come along."

Irritated and knowing that telling them no didn't work—they simply followed along at a distance— Jack nodded. "Okay, just give me a sec."

He turned and headed for the examination room, but realized he didn't want to leave them inside with access to his office. He whirled and headed back toward them. "Why don't you go ahead and wait for me in your van. Give you time to warm it up."

Marina nodded in agreement. "Sure. Good idea."

Her cameraman opened the door for her, and then Jack held it for him as he maneuvered the expensive video camera unit through the doorway. Jack closed the door, turning the lock as quietly as he could. He then headed straight for the examination room and out the other door that led out back, effectively ditching the news crew. His gut told him the last thing Ruby needed was to have her upset featured on the evening news. And it would be, because she was a fellow winner.

Besides, since he only had to pass Faulkner's Hardware and The Brimming Cup, then cross the side street Mayor Bobby Larson had had the ballocks to rename Big Draw Drive to reach the back of The Mercantile, he'd be shortening the time it took him to get there.

As he made his way along the backside of the Main Street businesses, which looked much smaller than they did from the front with their old-west style facades, all Jack could think about was how nice it would be to move some place where he could do his job without having to slip out the back door of his own clinic.

A place where no one knew who he was, or could remind him of his pain.

# *Chapter Three*

Melinda dragged her feet up the side porch steps to the little house she rented on Mega-Bucks Boulevard late that afternoon, weary to the bone. She should have been exhilarated after having her work praised as much as it had been by Wyla.

But when the thin, sour-faced woman wasn't complimenting Melinda on her veterinary skills, she was griping. From afar, of course. With plenty of hired hands to do the work, Wyla no longer went anywhere near the animals that her last husband had been forced to "give" her after a nasty divorce. But she still stood in the pig barn door and griped and griped. About everything.

Though she'd been smart enough to keep her complaints about Jack, and the insinuations she'd been making around town that he stole her money by opting into the lottery after she'd opted out, to the minimum. She must have known Melinda wouldn't stand for it. It was no secret he had her loyalty. Blessedly, the fact that he also had her heart remained a secret.

Wyla's negativity had simply beaten Melinda down

in a way wrestling several dozen pigs never could. She definitely couldn't wait to seek comfort with her critters over this day, and had come straight home after finishing up at Wyla's rather than stopping in at the office like normal. The paperwork, and Jack's talk, could wait.

How was she going to talk him out of leaving without revealing too much? She shook her head at the seeming impossibility and let herself into the house. She'd been told when she first moved here that she needn't worry about locking her doors. After the lottery win, however, the town sheriff, Luke McNeil, had advised everyone, even nonwinners, to take precautions. There were a lot more strangers in town now, thanks to its new notoriety.

The side door of her house opened right into a tiny laundry room. After she greeted her fat, notched-ear, half-blind, gray-and-black tabby cat and his timid, snow-white counterpart, per her routine, she stripped off her filthy and smelly work clothes—today the scent being *eau de hog*—and tossed them straight into the clothes washer. Down to her French-cut, cotton underwear and bra, she trudged through the little kitchen, the harvest-gold linoleum cold under her feet and the eager cats dangerous around her ankles.

She bought herself some safe-walking time by stopping to refill their food bowls, then went through the cozy living room to the short hall that the bathroom and her bedroom opened off from. Heading straight for the shower, she did her best to wash away the day behind a white with blue dog-paw print shower curtain.

The mud and manure were easy, requiring only a little soup and a nail brush. Wyla's negativity succumbed under the force of the massage setting on the shower head. Bud Webster's chauvinism required a few choice words that echoed nicely off the bathroom's white and blue-flecked tile. But no matter how hot or hard she ran the water, Jack's words, his pain, appeared to be with her to stay.

Turning pruney and needing to see to her other animals, Melinda gave up, turned off the shower and stepped out of the tub. She towel-dried her long curly hair as best she could, combed it out, then donned the pink satin pajamas and terry cloth, powder-blue robe with white clouds that she kept hanging from a ceramic cat's paw on the back of the bathroom door. Out of the pockets of the robe she pulled thick woolen socks the cats assumed were some other weird creatures she'd taken in. She put them on, then went to tend to the rest of her menagerie.

The cats had already been seen to, but her parakeet with the broken beak needed water and her barbecue-singed guinea pig needed more pellets in the cages in a corner of the living room. In the laundry room she slipped her stocking feet into oversize rubber boots and went out into the fenced backyard.

She saw to her three rabbits in their hutch next to the house, added fresh straw to her two pigmy goats' little shed to keep them warm through the very cold night, and coaxed her beloved, three-legged dog into the house. A mutt of some kind, mostly Australian shepherd she figured, he had been the first animal she'd rescued after moving out on her own, and his tenacity and good nature inspired her to keep at whatever she was doing no matter how tempted she was to give up. The silly thing loved to be outside in his doghouse, no matter how frigid the weather, but Melinda insisted he come in with her at night, as much for her and her need for company as for his health.

Kicking off her boots then reaching for an old towel to dry his white, black and brown coat, she met his warm, brown eyes as she rubbed the snow from him. "This was one of those days, Pete. I think even you would have stayed in bed."

He sneezed as if to pshaw her, then hopped away into the kitchen.

"Fine. Cats know how to pity." Melinda followed him, washed up, then made herself some soup, turning the TV on to the news while her dinner heated.

With her soup in a great big mug painted black and white like a Holstein dairy cow—a gift from her mother—Melinda went into the living room to eat. She cozied up on her dark brown, overstuffed couch and allowed the cats to settle in close enough to comfort but far enough away to keep their hair out of her soup.

She'd only taken two sips of the rich broth when the logo the local press, with the mayor's help, had come up with for Jester since the lottery win—Millionaire, Montana—flashed on the screen next to the anchor's head. Melinda rolled her eyes. Not again.

She knew there had to be more important things going on in the world than whatever piddling dirt they'd managed to dig up on the lottery winners.

Then a picture of the Jester Veterinary Clinic came up on the screen and gained Melinda's complete attention. The anchor started talking about Jack—or more accurately, the Big-Bucks Bachelor—and how he wasn't going to be a bachelor for long. Melinda gaped at the TV, stunned by what she was hearing.

Then they went to commercial.

Her heart stalled in her chest despite her brain's immediate attempt to scoff it off. But the panic hovering in the wings was unquestionable and terrifyingly intense. Could it have happened again? Could she have again fallen for a man who had eyes for someone else without her knowledge?

No. Jack couldn't be secretly involved with someone.

Mary Kay Thompson, sitting coyly on the exam table, came to mind. Melinda tried to reject the notion, but Mary Kay *had* managed to get rid of Melinda for a while. But why not just close the door if they wanted to fool around?

Melinda shook her head, sloshing her soup. No. Not Mary Kay. Not anyone. It couldn't be.

Still, she'd never experienced a more agonizing commercial break in her life.

The news came back on.

According to an unnamed source, the anchor continued, Jack Hartman—and they put up a picture of

him so there was no doubt it was *her* Jack Hartman—
was engaged to be married.

With the conversation of earlier today still ringing
in her ears, Melinda's brain won out. Jack hurt too
much to have moved on. A guilty relief rushed
through her so fast it almost made her dizzy. How
embarrassing for *that* reporter.

Then Melinda's picture, obviously taken from a
distance then enlarged, showing her hair flying in a
mess and a fierce look on her face, flashed on the
screen. And the news anchor, sounding extremely certain, announced that fellow veterinarian Melinda
Woods was the lucky gal to finally rope Jack.

Jaw slack, Melinda stared at the screen, oblivious
to the soup running onto her surprisingly absorbent
robe.

JACK STARED UNSEEING at the barbecue sauce he
stirred, thinking about the thieving stray dog he'd
capped his day off by failing yet again to trap. After
he had escorted the bucket-head billy goat from
Ruby's back room, freed it from its five-gallon hat by
docking its horns and turned it over to the kid who
owned it with a lecture on proper fencing, he'd gone
to check the trap that he and Luke had set for the dog
in the scrub bushes behind The Mercantile.

An awful lot of the townsfolk would simply prefer
the sheriff shot the dog, fearing it was a wolf. But
Luke, either because of his Native American heritage
or just the plain fact he liked animals, had come to
Jack instead. They'd managed to get close enough to

the animal to clearly see that it was actually a German shepherd-husky mix whose thick, grayish-brown coat made it look like a wolf at first glance.

Jack also had been able to see—as it hightailed away from them—that the dog, a male, had been neutered, so Jack knew it was simply a stray rather than a true feral dog. It had undoubtedly been abandoned by someone along the highway, because Jack knew that no one in or around town had ever owned a dog like that.

The mutt didn't deserve to be shot, especially since the worst it had done so far was tear into garbage bags and make a mess. And though he'd never admit it, deep down, he felt a strange kinship with the dog. They were both just a couple of strays.

So he and Luke had set up and baited a trap, but the dog hadn't fallen for it yet.

Jack glanced outside through the kitchen window, the view of the snow falling gently within the reach of his back porch light framed by the frilly white-and-blue checked curtains Caroline had sewn. If the weather continued to be this nasty, though, he was sure the poor dog would eventually have to take the bait.

He sighed and checked his watch, wishing he'd been on the ball enough to have thought to go back into his office and grab some paperwork that needed to be done before he'd slipped out on the news crew. But he hadn't imagined that they would camp out at the clinic waiting for him to show again.

Either way, Melinda would have taken care of what

had needed to be done in the office. Good thing, too. Those vaccines and medical supplies weren't going to reorder themselves.

The sauce bubbled up at him and brought him back to the task of making dinner. He normally didn't take the time to make himself a regular meal, but he'd been forced to come home early today, and he'd certainly had the time. Heck, he might as well go as far as to fix a salad. He ducked outside to check the chicken breast he was grilling on the back porch, turning the heat up to combat the freezing air temperature, then came back inside and went to the fridge to get salad makings.

A knocking—make that a *pounding*—on his front door stopped him. Annoyance flared to anger in his gut. He'd figured that if the news crew really wanted to talk with him they would eventually come to his house when he failed to show his mug on Main Street today. He'd just figured they'd be more polite about it.

He strode from the kitchen through the dining room to get to the front door of the house he and Caroline had bought when they moved to Jester. A lecture on manners poised on the tip of his tongue, he yanked open the door, then blinked in surprise when he found Melinda standing on the raised wooden porch that ran the length of the front of the house.

Her hair hung in long, dark ringlets, clearly damp, and while she had on her usual heavy coat, underneath she wore what looked like dark pink satin pajamas tucked into knee-high rubber barn boots. Her getup, coupled with the glitter of worry in her big brown eyes and the way she'd clamped her full bottom lip between her teeth sent Jack's heart straight into his empty stomach. Oh, no, what now?

"Mel, what—"

"Jack. Thank goodness you're here. I looked for you at the clinic, since your truck is still there, but it was empty and locked up, and I hadn't seen you anywhere on Main Street—"

Understanding dawned on him, along with a hefty dose of guilt. She'd thought something had happened to him. "Ah, Mel, I'm sorry to have worried you. Come on in out of the cold." He tried to usher her inside, but she took the time to step out of her barn boots, leaving them on the porch. He was momentarily distracted by the thick, fuzzy gray socks she wore. No wonder she'd had to wear those great big boots. Those socks wouldn't fit into anything else.

Once inside, he automatically reached to take her coat.

She unbuttoned the heavy coat and started to pull it off, but her attention was on the turned-off TV in the living room. "I'm guessing you didn't watch the news."

"No. I haven't had...it...on..." He trailed off when he caught sight of what was under her coat. He'd been right, she did have pajamas on. The top wasn't the slightest bit risqué—it had long sleeves and was buttoned all the way up to the collar, only slightly veed neckline—but the fluid satin skimmed her breasts, breasts Jack had noticed but had never given a second thought to. Now he was giving them so much thought he couldn't think about anything else. And he couldn't quit staring. He made a blind grab for her coat.

Apparently not noticing where his attention lay, she delivered the coat into his hand. "Well, you should have been watching the news."

That brought his gaze back to her face. Her expression was ominous.

"Why?"

"Because we were on it."

He groaned and went to hang her coat up in the nearby closet tucked beneath the stairs. "Jeez. I should have known dodging that news reporter and her cameraman wouldn't keep them from running some sort of story anyhow. That's why I'm here, but my rig is still at work. I ducked out the back door to keep from having to talk to them."

He should have at least found out what they wanted to talk to him about, rather than finding out about it after the fact.

"So you haven't talked to the newspeople at all lately?" There was an odd, strained quality to her voice.

Before he could consider why, he caught the sound of the barbecue sauce he was making for the chicken bubbling. He started toward the kitchen. "No. Not since they dubbed me the Big-Bucks Bachelor. They pretty much blew their chances with me after that."

He waved at her to follow him. "Come on into the

kitchen. Because I came home so much earlier than normal, I'm grilling some chicken.''

She screwed up her face. ''You're barbecuing? In this weather?''

''Of course I am. I'm a guy.'' He went to the stove and turned down the sauce, then glanced back at her pajamas, unfortunately noticing how her surprisingly full breasts moved beneath the satin. ''Have—'' his voice cracked and he jerked his gaze to her face. He cleared his throat and tried again. ''Have you eaten?''

She scoffed. ''I tried, but I'm afraid my robe ended up getting more of my soup than I did.'' She looked down at herself, as if checking for stains, and let out a soft gasp. She crossed her arms over her chest, flattening the fullness of her breasts.

He tightened his stomach muscles against his body's shocking interest. This was Mel, for God's sake. She was his partner, his co-worker, the professional he was going to leave his practice to. And she was the least appropriate person for his body to decide to come out of a five year dormancy for.

With a little, self-deprecating laugh, she said, ''I forgot I took my robe *off* because it was soaked. I guess I should have put some regular clothes on.'' Her gaze came back to his. ''But frankly, I wasn't thinking of anything besides talking to you. My gosh, Jack, you're not going to believe this.''

''Ever since Bobbie renamed the street I live on Lottery Lane, I'll believe anything, Mel.'' He picked up the wooden spoon to taste his sauce.

"Even that they announced on the news tonight that you and I are engaged to be married?"

Jack sprayed dark red sauce on the white tile back splash. "What?"

"They ran a story about how the Big-Bucks Bachelor, which would be you, isn't going to be a bachelor for long. And apparently I'm the lucky gal to have finally *roped* you."

"What the—where in blue blazes would they come…up…with…" He remembered what he'd said to Mary Kay only just that morning and slapped a hand to his forehead, his stomach folding in on itself with dread. "Oh, no."

Melinda's brows came together sharply and she uncrossed her arms. "What?"

His little lie couldn't have been blown so out of proportion so fast, could it? He shook his head, dismissing the notion. "No. It couldn't be from that."

She tucked her rapidly drying hair behind an ear and moved closer to him. He stupidly noticed how beautifully formed and delicate her ear was, how it so perfectly matched her dainty jaw and slender neck. No wonder some of the farmers didn't think she could handle their livestock.

Jack knew, though, that under all that femininity, which somehow, to this point, had been missed by him, was a woman as capable as the next guy. A woman who wouldn't appreciate being used by him to get out of an uncomfortable situation with another woman.

From low in her throat she said, "What'd you do, Jack?"

For the barest second he considered not telling her about what had happened with Mary Kay. But Melinda would learn of it eventually, or at least some mutated version of it. He pulled in a deep breath. "Remember when Mary Kay came in with Pumpkin earlier?"

She threw out a hip and crossed her arms again, this time unconsciously tucking them beneath her breasts and pushing them upward. He could see the deep cleavage that was formed where the neckline of her pajama top veed and left him with no doubt about the fullness of her breasts.

Jack's mouth went dry.

"Yes. She sent me schlepping out into the cold for no good reason. There was no icicle threatening my truck."

He ground his teeth as his previous annoyance with Mary Kay bubbled into something more serious. "I figured as much. She just wanted you out of there so she could try to jump me."

Melinda's brows shot up. "Excuse me?"

"She's trying to snag herself a millionaire. Any way she can. And as you've probably noticed, she's not the only one." He ran a weary hand through his too long hair. "It was kind of humorous for a little while. A *very* little while. But they're taking it too far."

Thinking of Paula Pratt, he added, "Anyone who would get a pet just to hit on a guy needs to have her head examined.'' He blew out a breath. "Anyway, Mary Kay wouldn't take no for an answer, and short of physically removing her from the premises—not to mention my body—the only way I could think of to put her off was to claim to already be involved with someone.''

Melinda's cheeks gradually became the same shade as her pj's. "How'd my name…''

"Mary Kay insisted on knowing who I was involved with.''

"So—so *you* said it was me?''

Guilt replaced his anger toward Mary Kay. "Yeah. You happened to walk by just then…'' He vaguely waved a hand, remembering the moment. "Besides, you're the only one who made sense. I mean, what other woman do I spend any amount of time alone with?''

She shifted her gaze to the sauce gently bubbling on the stove. "But we're just working.''

"You and I know that, but Mary Kay was obviously more than willing to believe there's been more than work going on. And for the record, I only said that we were seriously involved. I never said we were engaged. And I also asked her to keep it to herself.''

Mel made a noise. "Please. When I first moved here it only took me a matter of days to realize if you wanted to keep something a secret, you had to keep it to yourself.''

"I know, I know. I'll admit I wasn't thinking much beyond getting Mary Kay to leave me alone.'' He gave a slight shrug. "It did work, though.''

"Why didn't you just tell her you're leaving town?"

"I doubt that would have put her off. She'd probably be all over the chance to come with me."

Melinda made a noncommittal noise and picked up the spoon to stir the sauce.

Guilt made his back teeth ache. But what was done was done. "I suppose you're mad."

"I just want to know how we're going to straighten it all out. I mean, it's not just Mary Kay, anymore. And it's not just that we're *seriously involved*. Everyone thinks we're engaged." She looked up at him, her brown eyes soft and reflecting the warmth of the kitchen light. *"Engaged, Jack."*

He slapped a hand to his forehead yet again. Suddenly the rest of his day made sense. "Oh, man. Stella and Irene stopped by wanting to know my favorite kind of cake and slow song."

"You don't think they're planning our wed—"

He waved her off before she could finish. "No, no. They wouldn't take it that far." He silently prayed they wouldn't. To keep from worrying her further, he said, "I'm positive they only want to make sure that they have all the bases covered." He gave a rueful laugh. "Granted, they kept interrupting me, but at least they weren't throwing themselves at me."

Melinda turned and paced away, shaking her head, her long curls swinging down her back. "What a mess. How are we going to convince everyone it's all a mistake?"

A mistake that quite effectively got Mary Kay off

his back. And front. Would it work as well on Paula and the others? Granted, the existence of Bobby Larson's *wife* didn't keep Paula away from Bobby, but Jack figured the good ol' mayor had more than a little hand in that illicit relationship. And unlike Regina Larson, Melinda was always around, either handling appointments at the clinic or going to and from calls.

An idea bloomed in his brain. In the past six months, Melinda had proven she was someone he could depend on, and despite his newfound awareness of her physical attributes, he considered her a friend, first and foremost. A friend who might be willing to help him out. And anything would be worth getting at least some semblance of his routine back.

He planted his hands on his hips and watched her pace away. "Who says we have to?"

She stopped dead, but didn't turn around.

"Since the clock is ticking anyhow on my time here in Jester, what harm would there be in letting this whole misunderstanding ride for a while?"

She turned slowly toward him, her mouth gaping. Hopefully he wasn't about to send her packing from Jester faster than the chauvinistic farmers ever could. But the chance to be able to end the harassment and unwanted attention he'd received at the hands of the gold diggers in these parts was worth the risk.

Besides, after seeing how angry she'd been over Bud Webster not letting her treat his pigs, Jack figured Melinda sported a hefty dose of stubbornness. She'd want to stick around if only to prove Bud and all the other farmers and ranchers like him wrong.

Jack raised his hands and went to her. "Just hear me out. You know yourself how much the women like Mary Kay have been disrupting things at the clinic. But if we allow them to continue to think you and I are engaged, we can get back to being available to the animals who really need us."

In the hopes of reassuring her, he moved close enough to gently take a hold of her upper arms, her pajamas silky beneath his palms. He pushed the sensuous feel of the material from his mind, concentrating instead on the strength he knew was in the muscles beneath, on what a good sport—a good friend—he knew her to be. The faint citrus smell of her hair wasn't as easy to dismiss, though.

"So what do you say, Mel? Will you be my pretend fiancée?"

## Chapter Four

Melinda stared into the sweet-grass green of Jack's eyes and realized she had dreamed of hearing those words from him. In those fantasies, he'd held her gently in his strong arms, kissing his way up her neck to her ear, where he'd paused long enough to ask her to share the future with him. Though her dreams had been minus the word that sent a fence post through her heart.

*Pretend.*

He wanted her to be his *pretend* fiancée. Disappointment hit her as if she'd taken a hoof to the gut. He was dangling the one thing she wanted almost as much as she wanted respect for her work as a vet.

He wanted to use her to keep other women from chasing after him, from wanting to be with him. But none of them really wanted to be with Jack. Not the Jack who held tiny kittens in his big, strong hands, and cooed to them until they fell into a trusting sleep. Or the Jack who would place his muscular body between a frightened foal and the fence it was stuck in to keep the baby horse from further injuring itself.

Those women wanted to be with the hunky, rich, Big-Bucks Bachelor Jack. Or probably more accurately, they wanted to be with Jack's money. So she couldn't blame him for wanting to put up some sort of barrier against them, even if was just *pretend*.

So much wanting. And none of it meshed. She wanted Jack, the other women wanted Jack's money and Jack wanted to be left alone. It made the backs of her eyes burn.

She blinked fast and pulled away from him, moving closer to the stove. She couldn't let him see what his idea was doing to her insides.

His deep, soft voice, the voice that could convince a horse tangled in barbed wire to stand still, eased around her. "I swear I won't let Stella and Irene plan a wedding. And I'll definitely put the kibosh on any engagement party they might have tucked up their sleeves."

She turned back to look at him. He kicked up one corner of his sensuous mouth in an *it ain't no big deal, trust me* smile. He didn't have a clue about the kind of power he had over her.

Or how her heart would suffer.

His bright green gaze flicked over her embarrassingly practical pajamas. What a nitwit he must think her.

"It will only be until I leave, Mel."

Until he left, taking her heart with him.

Well, if she was going to help him, she'd dang sure get something in return.

She cocked her head and tapped a finger on her

chin. "Now, let me get this straight. You want me to lie to the good people of Jester just so you aren't pestered anymore by money-grubbing females. Is that what you're asking?"

He took a step toward her, unconsciously crowding her senses and effectively pinning her against the stove. A wave of heat that had nothing to do with barbecue sauce simmering in a pot behind her engulfed her and made it hard to concentrate.

"If you strip it down bare, yeah, I guess that's what I'm asking." The velvety tenor of his words had her heart galloping around in her chest.

She craned her neck back and stared up at him, unable to keep her gaze from tracing the strong line of his jaw, the defined contours of his cheek, before colliding with his breathtaking gaze. She swallowed hard and forced out, "And then when you up and leave," her voice hitched slightly, "I get left here looking all pitiful because you decided you didn't want me after all."

She shook her head adamantly. "Nope, I won't do that, Jack. I've had my fill of that sort of humiliation."

His light brown brows slammed together and he opened his sensuous mouth, but she stopped him with a raised hand. "Just hang on. What I *will* do, is be the one to send you packing. I'll be the one to end it."

His grin made her want to weep. "So you'll do it?"

"With one more condition."

"Name it."

"Now, don't get all excited just yet, Jack," she warned. "It's a big one."

He visibly reined in his relief. "Shoot."

"In exchange for me pretending to be your fiancée, you have to agree to stick around town until I earn," she pointed a finger at him for emphasis, "I repeat, *earn* the respect of the farmers and ranchers like the Websters."

He tightened his square jaw and crossed his arms over his broad chest, pulling the fabric of his denim shirt tight at his ample biceps. "That might be a long while, Mel."

She shrugged and agreed. "It's definitely a risk." Her emotions were too jumbled to tell if she hoped or dreaded that he would balk at this particular condition. She couldn't believe she'd had the courage to make it.

He pressed his tempting lips into a thin line, clearly not caring for her stipulation, then he pulled in a noisy, deep breath and gave a short nod of his head. "Since I know how bad you want it, I know you'll work your tail off to make it happen sooner rather than later. I agree to your condition."

Melinda was surprised by the lack of satisfaction she received from getting her way. But she didn't need a degree in human psychology, which she didn't have, to know why his agreeing to her terms didn't make her happy. With the realization of one dream, the dream of being respected for what she could do, would come the death of another. The dream of spending her life with Jack Hartman.

After stepping into his home she could no longer entertain the fantasy that he would eventually see her in a romantic light. All she had to do was look around his house to know that Jack was still in love with his late wife. The refrigerator door was covered with photos of the two of them held fast by whimsical goose and chicken magnets. Frilly curtains that had definitely been picked out by a woman graced the windows. Dried flower arrangements in baskets were tucked here and there.

Five years had passed since her death, but it looked more like she had simply stepped out for groceries.

At least pretending to be his fiancée until he left might give her a memory or two of her own to cherish after he was gone.

He extended his wonderfully callused hand to seal the deal, and she slipped her much smaller hand into his, the haven he provided her by the simple act of engulfing her hand in his grasp not lost on her.

Absorbing his strength and confidence, she looked him in the eye and said, "Oh, and one last thing, Jack. If we're supposedly romantically involved, you'd better stop calling me Mel."

THE NEXT MORNING, Jack whistled through his teeth as he pushed through the glass-paned mahogany door of the Ex-Libris Bookstore—thirty-year-old Amanda Bradley's personal rebuttal to the notion that a dinky, rough-hewn town was no place for a classy bookshop.

Despite the fact that only a wall separated her half of the large building from the ever rowdy Heartbreaker Saloon—which was exactly the type of joint you'd expect in a town like this down to the paintings of scantily clad ladies—Amanda had taken her space to a much higher level of decorating.

She'd put up wallpaper with stripes of little, light purple flowers—lilacs, maybe—and laid carpet that was a subtle dove-gray to temper the dark mahogany woodwork. In the back of the store was a small sitting area complete with two burgundy leather chairs and matching twin leather love seats, plus a little table covered with a lacy white cloth that usually held a tray of Gwen Tanner's pastries.

If you got thirsty, there was a small mahogany cabinet stocked with ivory china teacups, which Jack would get his fingers stuck in for sure if he ever dared to use them, along with their matching saucers. The electric tea kettle that sat on top was always good to go. A basket holding all sorts of tea bags never failed to be fully stocked.

Though he'd come in to pick up the books on animal husbandry—and one on how to handle pets turned wild—that he'd had Amanda order for him, Jack's gaze traveled over the dark mahogany bookshelves and tables piled high with books. He liked to spend his evenings reading everything from the classics to the latest releases, and Amanda's store was a blessing.

As were Gwen Tanner's pastries. Taking advantage of the fact that Amanda was busy behind the mahogany counter ringing up Wyla Thorne's purchase, he made a beeline for the sitting area. Gwen just happened to be unloading a fresh batch of her baked goodies onto the little table.

"Good morning, Jack," Amanda said as he went by.

"Morning, Amanda. Wyla." He ignored Wyla's glare. "And a good morning to you, Gwen. Do I have perfect timing, or what?"

Wyla snorted disdainfully behind him.

Gwen's pretty, green gaze darted past him, then came back to meet his with an *uh-oh* look. He shrugged, unconcerned, and snagged a powdered sugar-coated puff pastry. He popped it in his mouth. Wyla had made no secret about her feelings toward him since the win.

Gwen's expression warmed and she clearly fought a smile. "Say, Jack. I caught the news last night."

Amanda chimed in, "Me, too. Congratulations, you sneaky devil. I can't believe you and Melinda were able to keep something that big a secret!"

Wyla snorted again. While she was only in her mid-forties and toothpick thin, she sounded remarkably like a large old man. "Sneaky and thieving," she grumbled.

"Now, Wyla," Amanda half soothed, half warned, offering Wyla her books.

The older woman's thin face reddened until it was nearly the color of her short hair. "Don't *now Wyla* me, Amanda Bradley. You and everyone in this town knows his money should be mine. He stole it from me.''

Gwen stepped forward. ''Wyla! How can you say such a thing? You didn't want to play the lottery that week. Jack did. It's not his fault they won.''

Wyla's pinched cheeks turned mottled. ''I might have changed my mind. I might have! But he took my spot. His share of the win should have been mine,'' she ranted, looking from Amanda to Gwen right through Jack as if he weren't there. ''And you know what? I don't think him and Melinda are really engaged.'' Her bright, angry gaze finally connected with Jack's. ''I'm surprised that reporter wasn't able to figure that out.''

He forced the pastry down and held his breath, hoping his shock that she'd guessed the truth didn't show on his face.

Wyla narrowed her gaze and pointed her bony finger at him, making Jack hear the witch's theme music from *The Wizard of Oz* in his head. ''Melinda was out at my place just yesterday and didn't say a peep about any engagement. And we talked for hours! I can't think of once when I've seen the two of them together outside of their vet clinic. He's probably just figured out a way to get even more money by claiming to be getting married.'' She snatched the books she'd purchased from Amanda's hand and stormed out of the shop.

Jack blew out the breath he'd been holding as Amanda and Gwen simultaneously apologized for Wyla's behavior.

"Don't you pay her any mind, Jack." Amanda turned to pull a small stack of books from the shelf behind her.

"It's just sour grapes," Gwen proclaimed, handing him another powdered sugar-coated pastry.

Amanda came toward him with the books. "You and Melinda have done an amazing job of keeping your relationship under wraps, though."

Gwen concurred thoughtfully, "An amazing job. I certainly haven't noticed her wearing an engagement ring."

"Well," Jack dragged the word out, his mind racing. He decided the closer he stuck to the truth, the better. "Mel—er, Melinda really wanted to be more established around here as a veterinarian before we made our personal relationship known. You know, so it wouldn't affect the way she was perceived as a professional." He ate the pastry to buy time as he thought some more. "And as far as the ring goes, generally, large animal vets don't wear rings. The patients wouldn't appreciate it, and talk about a pain if the ring were to come off while—"

"We get the picture." Amanda handed him the books, presumably the ones he'd ordered. "But you *have* bought her one? For when she's not working?"

He stalled for more time by looking at the covers of the books, the last one featuring a picture of a particularly vicious-looking dog standing over a garbage pile. "Ah, of course. We picked one out at a jeweler in Pine Run. But they didn't have the stone we wanted, so we had to order it."

Gwen shoved a napkin that matched the lilac floral stripe on the wallpaper into his hand and motioned for him to wipe his chin. He balanced the stack of books in one hand and complied. Powdered sugar sprinkled onto the snarling dog book cover.

She let him know he'd cleaned himself up with an approving nod. "I can pick it up for you when I'm in Pine Run next week."

Jack quickly said, "Thanks, but that's okay. We'll take care of it. When it's ready. Which won't be for a while. Probably a long while. Since they had to order it—from a long way away." Man, he sounded like an idiot.

Amanda cocked her head at her friend. "What are you going to be doing clear over in Pine Run?"

Gwen returned her attention to arranging her pastries. "Oh, just some...stuff I have to do."

Needing to change the subject, and fast, Jack asked, "How much do I owe you for these, Amanda?" He nodded at the books.

Amanda headed for her cash register. "I've got the order slip right here. Let me add 'em up."

To Gwen, he said, "What do I owe you for that delicious puffed thing?"

Gwen smiled broadly at him. "The pastry is on the house." She picked up a couple more and wrapped them in a napkin. "And here, take these, too. Consider them a very lame engagement present. But you have to share those with Melinda."

Amanda giggled. "Ooh, powdered sugar to lick off each other. Yum."

Jack felt heat rising up his neck. What had he gotten himself into? He shifted the books to one arm and pulled out his wallet as he moved toward the register.

Both women were laughing now at his apparently obvious discomfort.

Amanda recovered first. "Everyone is so happy for you, Jack. This is just the best thing. Melinda is a very lucky woman."

The flush of embarrassment turned to the burn of guilt. He hadn't considered what the price of lying to the people he saw daily would be. He and Mel—*Melinda,* he mentally corrected himself—would have to do their damnedest to pull their little charade off so no feelings were hurt or friendships damaged. Thank goodness it wouldn't have to go on for long. If he hauled Melinda out on calls with him, they should be able to get her accepted by the old guard in no time at all.

Mumbling a thank-you of some sort, he paid for the books, then wished them a good day as he started out the door. Then something very important occurred to him and he stopped. "Hey, Gwen?"

She straightened away from the little table and her pastries. "Yeah, Jack?"

"Do me a favor?"

"Sure. What do you need?"

"Could you make sure that Stella and Irene don't plan any sort of engagement party, or anything of that...sort?"

Amanda and Gwen both started to protest at the same time, but Jack stopped them. "Now, hang on.

You guys know how shy Melinda is. She would really rather not have a party in our honor. Okay?'' He felt even more guilty about using Melinda's shyness as his excuse, but it was one he was sure would work. None of these women would dream of making someone feel uncomfortable.

Gwen heaved a sigh, and he received a corroborating nod from Amanda.

Gwen said, ''All right, Jack. I'll talk to Irene and Stella. But I can guarantee, whether they have something planned already or not, they'll be disappointed.''

Relieved, Jack said, ''I know, but it's important. Thank you.'' He continued outside.

The bookstore was directly across Main Street from the Jester Veterinary Clinic, but he still risked slipping on the ice and snow and landing on his can by breaking into a jog to get him there that much faster. He needed to talk to Melinda ASAP. Hopefully she hadn't left yet on a call.

They needed to make sure their stories jibed regarding their reasons for the secrecy and her imaginary ring. A game plan was also needed for how they were going to proceed. Certainly there would be other skeptics, and he and Melinda needed to start offering some proof of their relationship. Plus, the more they were seen together, doing couple-type things, the less likely it would be for Mary Kay and her type to think they could come between him and Melinda.

The idea of them being too close for anyone to squeeze in brought an image of Melinda in his kitchen to his mind and his body sparked annoyingly to life. He'd just have to make sure Melinda never wore her silky pajamas while they were doing things.

If all went well, the end result would be that he'd be left alone to do his job and live his life. For as long as he stayed in Jester.

# Chapter Five

Melinda looked up from the vaccination reorder forms she was filling out when Jack came blasting through the clinic door. He had a stack of books tucked under one arm and a purple flowered napkin wrapped around something in his hand. His gaze connected with hers, and his relief at finding her there was obvious in the devastating smile he flashed her.

"Thank goodness, you're here." He shut the door behind him and came into the office.

Melinda's heart sped up at the idea of Jack being so glad to see her. What other mind-blowing proposition could he have for her?

She cleared her throat. "I didn't have anything scheduled this morning, so I thought I'd help you out with this paperwork." And she'd been so nervous about seeing him on the first day of their *engagement* that she'd awakened well before her usual 6:00 a.m. only to torture herself with what to wear, for heaven's sake. To keep herself from putting on yet a different turtleneck, which was about all she owned that wasn't flannel, she'd come in to the clinic. "What's up now?"

"We need to get our story straight." He set the books down on his desk and shook his head. "I can't believe I didn't think of this last night. But with everything…" His gaze flicked over her, then away.

Melinda clenched her teeth. He'd probably been distracted by what a frump she was in her men's style pajamas and fuzzy socks.

As if remembering he held the napkin wrapped around whatever in his hand, he said, "Oh, and this is for you. From Gwen."

Melinda set the paperwork aside and reached for the napkin, her trepidation over what he might be talking about slowing her heart rate considerably. "Our story?"

"Yeah. You know, when I supposedly asked you to marry me, how, where, what the ring in Pine Run looks like…."

She paused unwrapping what she'd already guessed to be a pastry of some sort from the powdered sugar flicking onto the dark surface of her desk. "Ring?" There was going to be a ring? Her heart stopped completely. How was she supposed to remember that this was all pretend if he went and got her a ring?

He folded his large frame into his seat and pointed at the puffed pastries she'd uncovered. "I stopped in across the street. Gwen and Wyla were there, and Amanda, of course. Thanks to Wyla, they started asking questions." He sat back, blowing out a breath and ran both hands through his hair, carving paths through the thick, slightly waved locks as he massaged his head.

Melinda was momentarily distracted by the notion of what those hands would feel like in her hair. They were big enough that he could massage her whole scalp without much effort at all. It would be heaven on earth.

"They wanted details. Like had I bought you a ring." He grimaced. "I didn't realize how hard it would be to lie to them."

She blinked to focus and sat back in her chair also. "It's hard because you're not a liar." She had discovered right off when she started working with Jack and learned how he kept his books that he was as honorable as he was handsome. The fact that he was willing to deceive so many people with this false engagement drove home how important being left alone was to him.

And how unattainable he was.

He linked his hands behind his head and spread his elbows wide, pulling his shirt tight across his broad chest.

Melinda shifted in her seat. Dang her stupid body for being so responsive to every little thing about him.

Jack blew out a heavy breath. "Yeah, well, I'm going to have to be a damn good liar for a little while. It beats the hell out of taking a cattle prod to the gals like Mary Kay."

Despite the fact that she'd actually enjoy seeing him do that, Melinda clucked her tongue. "Noble intentions, wrongheaded execution. But I suppose it's too late to go back.'' She took a bite of one of the pastries, which turned out to be delicious. ''Mmm.'' Then she muffled around it, ''What'd you tell them?''

He recounted his conversation with the three ladies, getting her dander up when he told her how Wyla had started the whole thing by accusing him of stealing her money.

While she swallowed, Melinda thought of all the griping she'd had to listen to from Wyla. ''She's a real piece of work.''

He shrugged. ''She sure had my blood pumping when she said she didn't think our engagement was real.''

''You have to see her point. We haven't exactly, um, hung out together.'' It had always been just business with Jack. While she respected him for that, she couldn't deny the disappointment that went hand in hand with his *see ya tomorrow*s. She went home to her animals, he went home to his memories. It was a sad thing.

''I know. We need to change that. Big time.'' He took his hands from behind his head and leaned forward, a spark lighting his eyes as he clearly warmed to the challenge. ''We should eat out together, maybe even go to the movies. We should also probably *hang out* at the Heartbreaker every once in a while. Do a little slow dancing.''

Melinda's heart lodged in her throat at the prospect of being in Jack's arms, swaying to music, pretending to be pretending to care about him. She wasn't sure she could do it. ''Don't you think that's overkill?''

He leaned back in his chair again, his expression serious. "Like you said, I'm generally not a liar, so I'd prefer not to get busted on this one. There'd be too many hurt feelings. The more convincing we are as an engaged couple, the better."

Unfortunately for Melinda, the more convincing they were, the more likely her hurt would be something she'd have a tough time bearing when he left. She dropped her gaze to the partially eaten pastry puff. While she had experience in loving but not being loved in return, she'd always had a certain amount of indignation to get her through the aftermath. But Jack had done nothing other than show her respect. If he hurt her, it was because she allowed it.

"So," he regained her attention. "What sort of ring would you pick out?"

She pulled her chin back, surprised that he'd asked, let alone care. She looked down at her bare fingers. They were rough from being washed so often with strong, disinfecting soap and chapped from the cold. She'd have to add some lotion to her bag if people were going to start looking at her hands. "Something small and simple, I guess, like a narrow gold band. My hands aren't very big."

"I'd want to buy you a diamond."

The gravity of his tone made her jerk her gaze up to meet his and she was caught in the emotion-darkened intensity of his eyes. Before she could decipher if she saw longing or regret in his gaze, he shifted his attention to the photo of his late wife.

Melinda's heart curled in on itself as if it were a

sow bug. If only she had the same sort of hard, protective shell. But she'd known what the going would be like when she agreed to the ride. The sooner she toughened up, the better.

Jack waved off whatever he'd been thinking and looked back at her. "But it's your call. We need to settle on something, though, so we can give the same answer when we're asked."

She pulled in a deep breath and focused on the fine dusting of powdered sugar on her desk. "Okay. Well, let's see. People have certain expectations of you now that they might not have had before."

"What do you mean?"

She met his gaze, surprised that he could be so clueless. "They think of you as a millionaire, Jack."

He rolled his eyes.

His lack of pretensions made her smile. "So we probably should tell them that you bought me a diamond, but since we're...well, us—a couple of vets who are happiest out in the muck with the animals—"

He grinned his gorgeous grin and inclined his head in agreement.

"—we can still keep it simple. Like a solitaire with a wedding band."

He grimaced slightly. "I kind of made it sound like we picked out something unusual, something that had to be ordered from somewhere else. To buy time."

She refused to consider exactly how much time she'd have to live this fantasy come true of hers. "All right. Something unusual." She traced a finger through the sugar, allowing her mind to think the way it would if what they were discussing were real, the way she'd think if Jack returned her feelings.

An image of a beautiful ring formed in her mind. "A one carat marquise cut diamond with half carat emeralds on either side of it." Emeralds that would match Jack's eyes when the shadow of his wounded heart darkened them. She gave a start when she realized she'd drawn a heart in the powdered sugar, and hurried to swipe it off as she met his gaze to make sure he hadn't noticed what she'd done.

His gaze was focused on her face, a bemused look in his very green eyes. He cocked a brow at her, then kicked up a corner of his mouth. "So much for small, but that'll certainly work. Diamond and emeralds it is." He pushed to his feet and paced to the office door. "Now for the other particulars. I'm thinking I asked you to marry me in January, after I picked up my lottery money. That would make sense."

It did make sense, and was about as romantic as reordering vaccines. She needed to keep things as unromantic as possible, though, to get through this. She pursed her lips and nodded as if she were giving it some thought. "Okay. Where?"

"Right here, I guess. You and I haven't exactly been seen together anywhere else." He stopped and tilted his head at her. "Why is that, do you suppose?"

She resisted the urge to squirm in her seat, then ventured tentatively, "Because you never ask me to do anything with you?"

He grunted as a sort of acknowledgment. "You're

always so focused on the work, I guess it never occurred to me.''

She waved a hand and tried to look unconcerned, the whole while wondering how he could be so blind, but at the same time grateful he was. ''That's okay, Jack. The work is what's important to me.'' She'd have that statement tattooed on her forearm if she needed to.

''Which is why I like you so much.''

Heat roared up Melinda's neck to her cheeks. Jack had never stated so concretely that he liked her before. Goodness, it was like Christmas in February.

Looking very satisfied, he said, ''Okay. I think we're set.''

In an effort to cool her cheeks, not to mention her jets, she reminded herself that it was her work ethic he liked, nothing more. Trying to keep it all business, she asked, ''What about a wedding date?''

He rubbed his chin as he thought for a moment. ''I'd rather not get specific. No matter how far out we make it, someone is bound to mark it on their calendar with the intention of planning something.'' He paced back toward the desk. ''How about if we say that we're holding off picking a date until the hoopla about the lottery dies down. That'll buy us tons of time.''

Liking the idea of having a ton of time with Jack, she smiled up at him. ''Works for me.''

He returned her smile, his gaze warm on hers. Her temperature skyrocketed and her tan turtleneck became too warm. He was so incredibly handsome, so virile, so oblivious. Those women might be just after his money, but talk about bonuses.

She sighed and checked her watch. "I'd better get going." She stood and moved past him to the coat-rack. "You know that pony Finn Hollis bought last fall for his grandkids?"

Jack nodded. "Nice little Shetland."

She pulled on her coat. "It's one unhappy little Shetland, now. He figured out how to open the latch to the grain shed and was helping himself. They caught him before he foundered, thank goodness, but his gut is still hurting him. I told Finn I'd come out again today to see how the little stinker is doing."

"Poor fella. Do you think you'll be finished by lunch?"

She paused. "Should be."

"Do you want to meet me for lunch?"

Her heart stuttered. *It's just for show* she reminded herself. "I suppose I should." Despite the reminder, it was a struggle to keep the delight from her voice. She was actually going to get to spend time with Jack, socialize with him, enjoying his company and his caring. May wonders never cease.

"See ya at The Brimming Cup, then. Give Finn my best."

"Will do." She picked up her bag and hoped it was heavy enough to keep her feet on the ground as she left.

IT WOULD MAKE HER LATE for her lunch *date* with Jack, but Melinda stopped by her house on her way back from Finn's to change her shirt and fix her hair. Something she'd never worried about taking time for before, even when she'd been dating Eric. Which might explain why he'd had his eye open for something better.

No. She stopped the thought in its tracks as she pulled into her driveway. She refused to take the blame for that jerk.

Though she kept telling herself this lunch date with Jack was for show, she didn't see any reason to meet him smelling of a fat little pony with serious stomach issues. Besides, she'd decided the tan turtleneck she'd settled on this morning, while it went well with her hair, didn't look as good on her as the red one did.

So she bailed from her truck and blasted into the house through her side door. She startled her cats who were sleeping in their beds on the dryer and excited the dog who, because of how cold the day was, for once, was hanging out in the house instead of taking advantage of his doggie door to be outside. They weren't used to her coming home so early on a workday.

"No time to chat, guys. I got me a man to meet."

They all blinked at her like she'd lost her marbles, which she very likely had, agreeing to Jack's scheme in the first place. It was too late now, so she might as well look good while she acted crazy.

She yanked off her work boots and hustled through the kitchen, nearly missing the blinking red light on her answering machine. Backpedaling, her wool socks slick on the linoleum, she stopped in front of the phone with its built-in message recording machine and stared at it. Who would be calling her here during the day? Everyone knew that if they wanted to reach her on any day but Sunday, they needed to leave a message at the vet clinic. Even Jack never called her at home. The only person who called her here...was...

Mom.

On Sunday nights at 7:00 p.m. exactly, without fail or variation. A chill raced down Melinda's spine.

Something must be wrong. The chill turned to a soul-freezing dread. What if something had happened to her father? Mom had complained for years that he wouldn't take care of himself properly, but his stubbornness and pride kept him from admitting he was getting old. Could the decades of hard labor on the farm that he had refused to allow Melinda to help him run have finally caught up with him?

There was only one way to find out.

Her hand shook in a telling way when she reached to push the play button. As much pain as her father had caused her over the years for not loving her the way she needed him to love her, she didn't want him sick, hurt or... She pushed the thought away as if thinking it could make it true.

The message machine clicked and whirred, then her mother's clipped, efficient voice filled the kitchen. "Melinda, it's Mom. I'm sorry for disturbing you during the week—"

Melinda rolled her eyes. She'd told her mother time and again that she could call her anytime, but Mom insisted that Sunday evening worked for her, and became indignant if Melinda tried calling her at any other time or before her mom had a chance to call first. It was Mom's routine, and Melinda had finally learned to accept it.

"—but I just heard from one of the neighbors about a news report that aired last night."

Melinda's heart stalled, then sprang into a stampede of pounding in her chest. She hadn't considered for one second that her parents might see the story.

"I didn't see it myself, of course. You know I only watch the weather and farm reports. At any rate, please call me when you have a moment. Again, this is your mother. Bye." The machine clicked off, leaving the kitchen oppressively silent.

Melinda stared at the phone. Good heavens, what was she supposed to do now? She couldn't lie to her mother. There was no other option than to let her mom in on the charade. It wasn't as if Mom would be speaking to anyone in Jester any time soon.

Melinda would just stress the fact that she was helping her friend and co-worker, Jack, out so they could get back to helping the animals that needed them. It was no big deal.

*It was no big deal* she repeated to herself as she reached for the phone and dialed her parents' number. Mom would be getting Dad his lunch about now. Dad might even be in the kitchen, himself, though why it mattered, she didn't know. He might want to speak with her this time, because she was supposedly getting married....

Her mother answered on the second ring.

"Hi, Mom." Thankfully her voice held steady.

"Melinda! I didn't expect to hear from you for hours, yet. How's the weather there?"

"It's cold, Mom. And snowing. I think. The reason why I'm calling now is, I, ah, I had to stop by the house for, ah, something. Something I needed to do here at home." There was no way Melinda was going to tell her mother she'd come home to primp before meeting Jack. She hated admitting it to herself, let alone anyone else.

"I'm getting your father his lunch right now."

Melinda fidgeted at the mention of her dad. She couldn't believe how much she still wanted his approval. "Ah, yeah, I figured you would be. That's why I called. I thought maybe I'd get a chance to talk to both of you."

"But it's not a good time, Melinda. You know how your father doesn't like his routine disturbed."

"I know." But she'd always wondered how much of that stemmed from her mother's need for sameness. "I just thought this would be a good time to return your call and talk to you about my supposed enga—"

"It's really not a good time, dear. I only called you to let you know we'd heard the news and to pass on our congratulations."

"But don't you want to know—"

"We trust you to have made a good decision about your life, Melinda. We know you'll do what you need to do to be happy. Now, I really must go. And I suppose I don't need to call you this Sunday, since I've already checked in with you this week and know you're fine. You take care, now, and give Jack our best. Bye.'' Her mother hung up without waiting for a response.

Melinda stood there stupidly as the dial tone kicked on and hummed in her ear. She couldn't believe her mother hadn't wanted to know more about her engagement.

She blew out a weary breath as she hung up the phone. Actually, she could believe it. That's the way things were in her family. It was little wonder the closest bonds she'd ever formed were with animals.

She scoffed it off and headed for her bedroom to change.

But her mom and dad trusted her to make the right choice. So was she making the right choice in agreeing to Jack's charade?

If only she knew for sure.

What she did know for sure was that she couldn't let the fact that her and Jack's engagement wasn't real get back to her parents now. She'd rather have them think it ended with a breakup than risk them thinking she'd made a foolish choice.

She'd never earn their respect otherwise.

MELINDA'S HANDS were slick on the chrome handle when she pulled open the door to The Brimming Cup diner. Jack was already there. She'd seen him seated in one of the six booths against the big front windows when she pulled up in her truck. But thanks to the phone call to her mom and an inability to settle on a hairstyle, she was really late.

Feeling very self-conscious from this unaccustomed explosion of vanity and insecurity about her choices, she could only give Shelly O'Rourke, the newly married and always friendly owner of the diner, a small smile as she went by where the brunette stood behind the counter.

Shelly's smile was broad and a knowing sparkle lit her hazel eyes. She tucked her chin-length, dark brown hair behind her ear and said, "Good to see you, Melinda."

"Same, Shelly," Melinda returned softly. While she had on occasion come into the diner for breakfast, Melinda usually packed a lunch so she could eat it on the way to a call or at her desk while she did paperwork. She had treated Shelly's cat, though, and the old tabby tomcat gave them a connection, of sorts.

She paused and asked Shelly, "How's Sean Connery?"

"He's doing great. Spoiled rotten, as usual."

Melinda didn't doubt it in the least. "Good. He's a great cat," she said awkwardly and continued toward Jack.

Jack looked up from the printed list of the day's specials. His smile was far from shy. It actually seemed overly bright. He slid from the bench seat and stood. "Hey, Mel—Melinda," he greeted her when she reached him, then shocked the bejeezus out of her by bending and landing a quick kiss on her lips.

She would have choked on her own spit if she

hadn't caught the warning in his gaze. She took a quick, subtle look around. Every gaze in the place was fastened on them, clearly eager to witness her and Jack's inaugural foray into the realm of the romantically involved.

Ignoring the tingling his lightning-fast peck had left in its wake, she looked back at Jack and reassured him with a bright smile of her own as she slid into the booth. Thank goodness the red of her top would blend with, and hopefully make unnoteworthy, the fiery heat she could feel in her cheeks. But Jack had been right to kiss her. If they were going to convince people that they were really involved, they'd better act like it.

At least he hadn't *really* kissed her, with any kind of depth or emotion. She probably would have fainted dead away on the spot if he had. There was no doubt in her mind that Jack could perform some serious magic with that mouth of his if he put his mind to the task. The sort of magic her imagination had tortured her with on many occasions, usually late at night in her lonely bed.

He moved to sit down again on the opposite side of the booth from her, but stopped himself, glancing around them much the way she had. Instead of reclaiming his original seat, he stepped to her side of the table and slid into the booth next to her, his hips and thighs bumping into her as he continued to scoot toward her as she scooted as fast as she could on the light blue vinyl.

Very crowded by his big body and aware of the

heat radiating through his shirt and jeans, she none-theless smiled. She should enjoy this, she reminded herself. Moments like these were her one and only chance to be close to Jack.

He met her gaze and shrugged. Leaning his head close, he murmured, "It's probably overkill, but everyone has been dying for you to get here after I mentioned you'd be joining me."

She nodded mutely. He was close enough that she could smell the spicy remnants of his aftershave min-gled with the warm, musky male smell of him over the sharp scent of the antibacterial soap they always used to wash their hands.

Even with talking to her mom, stopping by home to freshen up had definitely been a good call. Not only did she now look collected and capable, but she wouldn't make Jack wish he'd picked a different woman for his little charade.

The thought that he could have easily accomplished his goal with someone else sobered her considerably. Her name had popped out of his mouth because he liked her—as his partner in the veterinary practice. Keeping that in mind would make it easier for her when he left. She hoped.

Shelly came up to them beaming. "Hey, you two. Congratulations! I can't believe you were able to keep something so big such a secret. I'm impressed."

Being one of the *Main Street Millionaires* and hav-ing had a baby left on her doorstep by a local teen, Shelly undoubtedly knew firsthand what a spotlight Jack had been living in for the past couple months.

But she'd still managed to find love with the town's new doctor, Connor O'Rourke, and had maintained a big enough heart to take the teenager, Valerie Simms, in and give her a job here at the diner. The playpen tucked in the corner was for baby Max to play in when both Shelly and Valerie were working. Today Valerie must be home with baby Max.

Shelly had always been very kind and friendly toward Melinda, too. Unfortunately, talking to people was hard for Melinda. Focusing on her work was easier, safer. But for Jack's sake, Melinda met Shelly's warm hazel eyes and gave a similar version of the story he'd told Amanda and Gwen this morning. "We wanted people to get to know me as a vet before they started thinking of me as Jack's fiancée."

Shelly gave her a reassuring smile. "Trust me, people will still think of you as *you,* whether you're hooked up with this stud muffin or not." She gave Jack a playful shove that sent him rocking against Melinda.

He was so warm and solid Melinda had to fight the urge to wrap her arms around him to keep him there.

Jack laughed and straightened, taking the ribbing good-naturedly. "Say, Shel, has that stray dog been in your dumpster lately?" he asked, deftly changing the subject.

Taking out her order pad, she shook her head. "Not since I started leaving scraps for it. Though it won't come near them until I've gone back inside."

"Shelly! No wonder I can't get him to take the bait in the trap."

She shrugged guiltily. "I can't help it, Jack. The poor thing looks like it's starving."

"Which is why I'm trying to trap him, Shel."

Shelly grimaced. "Sorry, Jack. I'll stop."

"Thank you."

"What can I get you two lovebirds for lunch?" Shelly did a little subject changing, herself.

Jack nodded for Melinda to go first, pressing back against the booth so she didn't have to lean around him to be heard. His gentlemanly behavior wasn't lost on her, and she flashed him a quick smile as she ordered one of Shelly's fancy gourmet sandwiches that she occasionally tacked on to the traditional diner fare.

His turn, Jack said, "It's Friday, right?"

Shelly nodded. "All day."

He smirked. "Then I'll have your clam chowder."

"Daily special, it is. Congratulations again, you guys," Shelly said before she took their order back to Dan, her cook.

Jack readjusted himself on the padded seat and crossed his arms on the gray Formica tabletop. "I feel a little better now knowing why my trap hasn't worked."

Melinda nodded. Though he hadn't said much about it, she knew Jack had considered his inability to capture the stray an affront to his skill as a veterinarian. "He hasn't been hungry enough to risk going in after the bait. But once Shelly stops leaving him scraps, it shouldn't be too long before he goes after it."

"But Shelly isn't the only softy in town. I can't believe it didn't occur to me that people might be feeding him in some way or another. Probably because he's pretty fierce looking."

"Huh. Some want that stray shot because they think he's a wolf, and some want to feed him because they think he's a pitiful dog. It's all about perception, I guess."

He dropped his chin and looked at her, drawing her into the green fields of his eyes. "Kinda like how the Websters won't let you vaccinate their hogs because all they see is a pretty young woman too delicate for the job, while Finn made a point of calling me right after you left his place to tell me how great you were with his grandkids' pony. He said you're small enough not to spook the animal but no-nonsense enough to let it know who's boss."

The praise warmed her ears. Thinking of her father's unwavering convictions and her lifelong failure to make a dent in them, she asked, "Do you think it's really possible to change someone's perception?"

He shrugged, and moved his leg, his hard thigh coming to rest against her knee.

Every muscle from the point of contact all the way to her jaw tightened in response. Her body didn't seem to get the message that they were pretending, either.

"With a skill and knowledge of animals like yours, it's a sure bet." He sounded so certain. No wonder he'd agreed to her conditions. He figured he'd have her accepted and be out of here in no time. His praise suddenly became bittersweet.

Before she could decide if she should thank him or argue with him, old Henry Faulkner, with his sparse gray hair unkempt, his glasses smudged and his clothes wrinkled, came into the diner and headed directly to their table. Despite being seventy-seven years old, Henry was one of Jack's good friends—another connection to the town he seemed unaware of. Henry's grin was wide and looked heartfelt—something Melinda couldn't recall ever seeing from Henry before.

He'd always struck her as melancholy, despite the camaraderie he shared with Finn and Dean Kenning while they sat inside Dean's barbershop every afternoon. Like Jack, he was still mourning the death of his wife, who had passed away ten years ago.

But unlike Jack, Henry had let the loss of his wife affect more than just his heart. He clearly didn't take care of himself, and despite being one of the lottery winners and all the time he spent with good friends either in Dean's barbershop or here at the diner, he didn't seem to enjoy life much.

Henry slapped a frail-looking hand down on Jack's shoulder. "Jack, my boy! I just heard the good word. Price I pay for napping during the evening news, I guess. But I couldn't be happier for you, son. Nope. Couldn't be happier. Dolly would have been pleased, also." He patted Jack's shoulder. "About damn time, too, if you ask me. Salt of the earth fellow like you."

Henry gestured to Melinda with his other hand, his

watery eyes glowing. "And she's cute as a bug. Just be careful not to squash her, now."

Melinda fought not to roll her eyes, knowing he meant well. Jack's face was turned mostly toward Henry, but the cords of his neck stood out, like he had his jaw clenched tight. He probably didn't like the notion of lying to such a good friend. He'd started the charade, though, so he'd have to find a way to deal with the guilt.

Personally, she didn't like the taste of it. Her goal was to get these people to respect her, yet here she was disrespecting them in one of the worst ways possible. Jack might have started the charade, but now that she'd signed on, that she'd in essence lied to her own mother, she bore equal responsibility. They had to make it work.

Henry chuckled at his own joke, then patted at Jack's shoulder. "I'll let you kids alone and head back over to my spot at Dean's, but I wanted to tell you I'm glad. Damn glad. You're too young to end up like me."

Henry shuffled off, and she waited for Jack to say something, but all he did was glance at her, his expression unreadable before looking away again. She wanted to reassure him that they'd make their sham engagement work for everyone's benefit, but she couldn't come up with the right words.

Instead she pried her hands apart from where she'd been clutching them in her lap and lifted one to cover his large hand. She worked her fingertips beneath his palm. Her hands were far from smooth, but the rough ridges on his palm from calluses and scars reminded her of the hard shell Jack had encased himself in, and how difficult it would be for anyone to crack through.

If only she had more confidence in her ability to do it.

But just as she gave being his partner in the vet clinic her all, she'd give him her all in convincing the town he was off limits to marriage and or money-minded women. Despite the cost to her heart. She couldn't afford not to.

She squeezed his hand to show what she couldn't express with words, and he turned to look at her. His eyes were troubled. A look she'd never seen from him before. She squeezed again and gave him a small, understanding smile.

He responded by leaning in and giving her another quick, light kiss on the lips. It was clearly a kiss of thanks, nothing more, but it struck Melinda straight through the heart. Her eyes burned in a prelude to tears, so she looked quickly away. She couldn't add to his troubles by revealing how much he affected her.

The reality of Jack's physical attention, no matter what the motivation, was so much worse to bear than she'd imagined, because it was so much better than the fantasies she'd entertained these past months.

Heaven help her if she wasn't strong enough to handle the loss when he eventually walked away.

# Chapter Six

Jack hesitated as he stood on Mel's little concrete front porch preparing to knock on the shiny finish of the door, painted blue to match the trim on the boxy white house. They'd decided after lunch that, since it was Friday, they should be seen out together that night. The movies seemed the logical choice.

While Pop's Movie Theater, which happened to be right next door to their vet clinic, didn't usually run films until they'd been out for a while, and one of its two screens was patched with duct tape, it was still a popular destination for the dating crowd. The crowd Jack hadn't ever been a part of in this town.

Though he didn't mind in the least the idea of watching a movie with Melinda, he couldn't shake the sense of betrayal he'd harbored all day after Henry Faulkner had expressed his approval of Jack's supposed engagement.

Henry, and Stella to some extent, was one of the few people who understood why Jack was choosing to live his life the way he was, who knew from first-hand experience how he felt. How often had Henry sat in Dean's barbershop and convinced Jack that the empty, hollow feeling that consumed him the minute he walked through his door at home was mourning? That nothing would make it go away, so he might as well embrace it?

Henry and Stella had lost their partners in life and had decided to continue on alone.

Jack had thought for sure that he'd be forced to pull Henry aside and tell him the truth about the engagement because he'd assumed Henry would disapprove. Or at the very least, want to talk to Jack about his decision and make certain he knew what he was doing. But Henry hadn't. Just the opposite. He'd wholeheartedly approved of the engagement, wishing them all the best. Jack felt more than a little deserted by Henry.

If everyone was so damn eager for him to move on, he certainly should. To another town. A town that didn't hold so many memories of the life he was supposed to have had.

Jack set his jaw and rapped his knuckles on the door. Inside, a dog started barking excitedly and a bird of some sort squawked. Then he heard what sounded like someone running back and forth. A cat yeowled in pain and Melinda cried out. The dog's bark grew more excited. Jack could hear her talking to the animals, and although he couldn't make out her words, he could tell she was shushing the dog and soothing the cat.

Melinda yanked open the door, holding a large white cat tucked against her with one hand. She released the doorknob to make a grab for what turned out to be a black, brown and white three-legged shepherd mix.

He knew she'd had a rabies shot to administer not much more than a half hour ago, but she'd changed yet again into black jeans and a snug, ribbed, white turtleneck that drew his attention to her full breasts like her pajamas had.

Damn. Life with Melinda had been much easier before the fact that she had incredible breasts registered with him. He cleared his throat and yanked his gaze upward.

She had her hair down, something he'd only seen that one other time. Now it was dry, and her long, dark blond curls made her look like a mermaid, or vestal virgin, or something. And it had the same hardening, heating effect on him as her breasts had.

With her color high and her big brown eyes even more noticeable than usual, she looked exactly like a young woman ready for a date. Warning bells sounded in his head, but he shrugged them off. Melinda was *not* like those other women, after a man simply because he had a fat bankroll. She was too focused on proving herself as a vet to be thinking about a relationship. She was playing her part, that was all.

With the dog under control and no longer barking, just wagging its tail and trying to lick Jack despite being two feet away, Melinda looked up and flashed him a smile. "Hey, Jack. Come on in." She backed out of the way.

While he had suggested she take a look at this house when she'd been looking for something to rent after she'd accepted his partnership offer, he'd never visited her here. Never had cause to. Feeling more than a little strange about taking this step into her private life, he came inside. "Sorry to create such a commotion."

"It wasn't you. I was running around trying to get my act together and I stepped on Mr. Booger, here." She gave the cat, his tail twitching irritably and his yellow-green eyes glaring, a quick snuggle and a murmured apology then set him down next to a fat, black-and-gray tabby on the back of the overstuffed, dark brown couch that she'd used to separate the small, cozy living room from the entryway. "He insists on weaving between my feet when I'm walking around. It's the only assertiveness he ever shows. I've tripped over him or stepped on him enough, you'd think he'd learn."

Thinking that being nuzzled by a woman like Melinda wouldn't be such a bad fate, Jack said, "He probably figures your attention is worth the risk."

She shrugged, but her delicate mouth curled up and her expression softened as she gave the cat one last stroke. Turning her attention to the other cat, who was asleep despite the commotion, she said, "I'm a little embarrassed to tell you who this guy is. But I guarantee he was named long before I knew you."

Jack looked over the large, raggedy-eared, black-and-gray striped cat. "Let me guess. His name is Jack."

"One-Eyed Jack, to be precise."

At the sound of his name, the cat did indeed open only one eye to see what he might be getting. The lids of the other eye had been sewn shut. A bisecting scar gave proof of the necessity.

Jack ran his thumb gently over the big cat's scar. "Cat fight?"

She nodded. "Pretty sure. And no one in the neighborhood where he was found would claim him. I call him One-Eye now, to avoid any confusion."

A little disconcerted over being confused with a cat, Jack nodded mutely.

"This fellow here," she squatted next to the dog, who finally stopped pulling on his collar now that he was certain he'd get attention, "is Pete."

"As in Three-Legged Pete?"

She grinned and shook her head. "As in Peg-Leg Pete. Not that he has a peg, per say, but..." She gently lifted what was left of the mutt's left hind leg. "I left him as much as I could for balance." Standing, she ruffled the dog's think fur and let him come say hello.

Jack automatically dropped to one knee and ran his hands over the dog, noting several lumps and irregularities. "A car?"

She nodded again. "Really did a number on him. But he's a stubborn cuss. Refused to die. Sadly, his owners didn't want him afterward. They didn't want to deal with his recovery, so he came to live with me. Pete was my first rescue."

Jack stood, noting the two wire cages set atop an

antique buffet in the corner of the living room. "The first of many?"

She laughed, a very feminine sound that stirred something very male in him. "Only when absolutely necessary. Fortunately, it hasn't been necessary since I've been here in Jester." She led him over to the cages.

Jack approached the cage containing the motleyest looking guinea pig he'd ever seen. It was only sporadically covered with tuffs of white-and-brown hair, but on closer inspection he could see that the exposed skin looked scarred and there was evidence of other damage. His mood sobered and he reflexively clenched his fist. "A blow torch?"

Her smile faded and her velvety brown eyes hardened. "Barbecue. Some stupid teenagers bought her just for that. Thank goodness for nosy neighbors." She stuck her finger through the cage and gently scratched the guinea pig's cheek. It made soft little squeaks of pleasure. "Her name is Marshmallow."

Jack choked on a halfway-appalled laugh. "I suppose that, too, is appropriate."

Pointing at the next cage which held a small greenish-yellow parakeet, she said, "This little guy made the mistake of trying to steal a nut before his owner was done cracking it with the nutcracker. Lost part of his beak in the process. His name is—"

"Let me guess. Pecker?"

"No! It's Pistachio."

"I thought pistachios came already cracked?"

"Not all of them. Plus he's sort of the color of

pistachio pudding.'' She made kissing sounds at the bird, who responded in kind.

The sight of her puckered lips sent a crazy zing through his stomach and the pleasure her humor brought him made him warm. Trying his best to ignore this new awareness of her, Jack said, ''No wonder you don't feel the need to hang around Main Street during your off hours. You have plenty of friends right here.''

''Oh, these aren't all of them. I also have two pygmy goats and three rabbits out back. But I won't make you meet them. I don't want you to mess up your spankin' footwear.''

Jack glanced down at his boots. Despite the snow and ice, for God only knew what reason, he'd put on his dress cowboy boots. People were sure to believe he was serious about Melinda when they caught sight of him wearing these. A guy didn't put on his good boots for just any female. And from what he'd learned so far tonight, Melinda was far from being just any female.

*Don't forget you're leaving, Big-Bucks.*

He shrugged off the reminder and waved her concern away.

She went to the little, round oak table in the dining nook off the kitchen where she'd set her keys and lifted her coat off the back of one of the chairs. ''And we should probably get going so we don't miss the beginning of the movie.''

''The curiosity will kill me, though, if you don't

tell me the names of the rest of your animals and the reasons for them.''

She sighed. ''All right. But I'm beginning to think you're making fun of me.''

''Me? Never. I happen to know what tools you have at your disposal and what their uses are.''

She grinned wickedly at him. ''A good pair of snips do give a girl a certain amount of power, don't they?''

''Yes, ma'am.'' He went to her and took the coat from her hands and held it up for her to slide into. ''So tell me the names of the rest of your animals. All of which, I'm assuming, were also rescued?''

She eyed him and her coat for a second then turned to slip her arms in. He normally stood a head taller than her, but with the added height from his cowboy boot heels, he really towered over her. He still caught a whiff of the citrus-scented shampoo she used, and he couldn't help bending down a bit to really get a noseful. She reminded him of his last trip to Florida to visit his folks. Nothing but sunshine and orange trees. A place to visit, but not stay.

''Yes, they—'' She glanced back at him, obviously surprised to find him so close, and he had to pretend he was bent toward her to simply help her get her coat on easier. He didn't want her to think that he expected more from her than what she'd agreed to. He settled the coat on her shoulders and stepped back.

She looked away, then continued. ''They were in need of a good home. The two goats are named Willie Bite and Betty Won't.'' She held up a hand before he could open his mouth. "Trust me, you'll know within two seconds of being near them which one is Willie. He took one too many chunks out of his owner's backside and wore out their welcome. The bunnies are Thump, Bump and Roll. They were tossed out of car while in a sack."

"As if I didn't know it before, I'm now certain you've got a good heart. Plus you apparently have quite the talent for finding a little humor in some pretty grim situations."

"It was the animals who chose not to give up. I just give them the love they deserve. And now you know why I needed to find a practice to work at in a fairly rural area. Let me unlatch Pete's doggie door so he can go out if he needs to, and check everyone's food and water, then we can get going."

Jack watched her walk through the kitchen to a utility room, wondering about this new side of his partner. He'd known she loved animals. As a vet, that was a given. But he never would have expected this angel-of-mercy side of her. She took in wounded creatures and gave them the love and care they needed. He admired the hell out of that.

Especially considering not all wounded animals could be saved. How many had she adopted into her heart only to lose them anyway? He knew too well how much loving could cost someone. It was a risk he refused to ever take again. But Melinda had clearly been willing to take it over and over again. She had courage, that's for sure, and he admired that also.

He glanced around her little house. Her furnishings

and decorating weren't what he'd expected, either. She was so focused on her work that he'd thought her home would reflect that, also. That there would be less homey, decorator like touches such as the rich-looking tan drapes hanging from wrought-iron rings on a matching rod, or the inviting, overstuffed couch and armchair covered in a dark brown fabric that begged to be plopped down on with a beer and the remote.

And in true girly fashion, there were candles, accent pillows, throw blankets and mail-order catalogs everywhere. The tables looked antique, but not the hand-me-down sort, more like found treasures.

Framed photos hung on the walls, none professionally taken. A smiling older woman with familiar looking big brown eyes standing at a picket fence next to a dour looking slender man with short, curly blond hair. A little girl with a riot of blond ringlets grinned from ear to ear as she sat perched atop a huge hog.

She *did* know from pigs.

Yet there was so much more to her than he'd originally thought. More to admire, more to like.

*Uh-oh.*

She came back through the kitchen freeing her hair out from beneath her coat. Once she had it pulled out, she released her hair, and it cascaded down onto her shoulders in a mass of dark gold curls. Jack's mouth went dry.

Okay, so now he knew why he'd put his good cowboy boots on. And he doubted he'd have any trouble thinking of her as Melinda instead of Mel from now on.

EVEN THOUGH the two movies showing at Pop's Movie Theater were probably already available on video somewhere, there wasn't much to do in Jester on a wintry Friday night, so Jack and Melinda had plenty of witnesses to their *date*. He played it up by holding her gloved hand as they waited in the thankfully short line to buy their tickets, accepting congratulations right and left.

He couldn't tell if it was the icy wind or embarrassment that kept Melinda's cheeks a becoming rosy red. And he couldn't believe that he'd never really noticed just how pretty she was, especially with her hair down and blowing around her face like a gorgeous golden cloud.

She finally asked, "What?" because he kept glancing at her.

He mumbled something incoherent and headed straight for the refreshment counter.

Having forgotten how much great junk food was available at the movies, Jack loaded up on popcorn, candy and soda pop, much to Melinda's obvious amusement. Despite plenty of offers of seats from those who undoubtedly wanted to be close enough to see if any shenanigans went on between the town's vets, he and Melinda settled into seats a little off from center of the theater. In unspoken agreement they chose ones with enough space around them that they could talk without being overheard.

Unfortunately, the movie they'd decided to see was being shown on the screen with the duct tape-patched tear. But the action film wouldn't make them as uncomfortable with their situation as the romantic comedy playing on the undamaged screen would have. Though neither one had actually expressed the sentiment, it was obvious by how quickly that film was rejected by them both despite its better reviews.

Once they figured out who would hold what snacks, Jack slumped down in his seat, purposefully leaning toward Melinda so they looked snuggled up like a couple of teenagers. That should put the doubters at ease.

After swallowing a mouthful of buttered popcorn, he said, "You know, this isn't too bad."

"No, it's not. As long as nothing good happens right about there." She pointed a red licorice stick at the duct tape.

Her sense of humor sparked a long-dormant playfulness in him. "You mean, right…there?" He threw a piece of popcorn at the screen, well over the heads of the few people in front of them.

She gasped and slipped down in her seat as if to hide. "Jack!"

The other moviegoers chuckled. "Hey, Doc! You'd best settle down there," someone joked in a mock voice of authority.

Jack played along and whined, "Aah, man."

Pleasantly surprised by how much he was enjoying himself, he propped his arm on their shared armrest and noticed how Melinda moved hers off the moment they made contact. She seemed more than a little self-conscious. He figured that even without his popcorn throwing, they were the topic of more than a few whispered conversations going on around them in the partially filled theater, but he was surprised it affected her so. He shouldn't be. Melinda was a shy, quiet woman. And their relationship was fake.

He leaned toward her and whispered, "You okay?"

"Oh, yeah, sure," she insisted, becoming very interested in the straw in her soda.

Jack remembered something she'd said when they were hammering out the details—make that, conditions—of their agreement. At the time, he hadn't thought much of it, but now he realized he should have pressed for details then and there. The movie was bound to start any moment, but he figured he'd better try to find out as much as he could right away.

He leaned still closer to her, the citrus smell of her shampoo more enticing than the buttered popcorn. "Hey, ah, the other night you mentioned something about having had your fill of humiliation. What happened?"

She blinked at him. "Talk about *now for something completely different*. I certainly didn't get tossed out of a theater for throwing popcorn, if that's what you're wondering."

He grinned at her dry wit, but pressed, "No, I kind of figured it had something to do with a guy. A guy you were involved with. Am I right?"

She glanced around, as if making sure they were

still far enough away to not be overheard. They were. She sighed. "Yes, you figured right. I dated this other veterinary medicine student for a couple of years. I thought we were exclusively involved. Seriously involved." Her voice held a tremor that made Jack's insides clench.

She pulled in a breath. "He didn't. At least not after something better came down the pike." She held up a hand when she saw him open his mouth to argue with her perceptions. "His words, not mine. Delivered in a very public place—the student union hall— when I came across them playing kissy face and asked what the hell was going on. People talked about it for weeks."

Anger swelled in Jack until the popcorn bucket started to collapse in his hand. "Where does he live now?"

She shrugged. "Don't know, don't care. Why?" she asked before taking a supposedly nonchalant sip of soda.

"Because I'd like to go dent his face."

Soda spurted out of her mouth. She laughed and wiped at her chin. "Not that he doesn't deserve it, but your hands do too much good around here to risk injuring them on his stupid face. But I appreciate the sentiment. I really do."

"Please tell me you at least dumped soup on his head, or something."

She shook her head. "No. And sadly, I hadn't taken the course on neutering yet, either."

Jack chuckled despite his outrage on her behalf. "That jerk would be in trouble today."

"Yes, he would."

Heated to the core with the unexpected surge of protectiveness he blamed on the depth of their friendship, Jack lifted his arm and slung it around her shoulders.

She hesitated a moment, but when he pulled her toward him, she relaxed and leaned against him. She smelled so damn good, so welcoming. And she was delicate, yet solid enough that Jack didn't worry about crushing her with the weight of his arm.

A very primal part of him knew she'd be just fine beneath the weight of his body, also, but he squashed the thought the second it formed.

He gave her a squeeze and vowed, "I'd never humiliate you like that, Melinda. Never in a million years."

"I know, Jack." She pulled in a noisy breath and relaxed her head against his arm. "I know."

As if on cue, the lights dimmed completely and the trailers for coming attractions that had already come and gone in most cities flickered onto the screen.

And even as he snuggled her tight against him, rationalizing that he was just comforting a good friend who'd been treated poorly, the whisper of a warning started in his head. He had to be careful, because no matter what, Melinda didn't deserve to be hurt ever again.

Especially by him.

## Chapter Seven

For Melinda, the end of February and the first week of March were a torturous combination of heaven and hell. Her heart wept over her and Jack's newfound closeness, knowing it was just an act, a part he was playing to keep other women at bay. But she reveled every time he draped an arm around her when they walked to the diner for lunch or opened the truck door for her when they went out on calls together.

He made her feel special. No man had ever made her feel that way. Her father had wanted a boy, Eric had wanted someone better—in what way, she had no idea. But Jack made her feel good about who she was by doing the simplest things for her.

So far he'd also been holding up his end of the bargain, pushing her on the ranchers and farmers as much as he could to show them what she was capable of, reassuring them that she could easily do the job as well as he could. But while he was around, many of them still insisted on deferring to him, acting as if she were nothing but his assistant. While their lack of respect gave her more time with Jack by keeping him in town, she often came back from a job with an aching jaw from gritting her teeth in frustration.

After one such call where they failed to convince Bud Webster to let her do more than ready the vaccine for Jack to administer, Jack suggested they go home to clean up, grab a bite to eat, then head over to the Heartbreaker Saloon for a beer. Melinda rushed to get ready because Jack had insisted on picking her up under the guise of yet another *date*. She hadn't actually done enough work to get dirty or work up a sweat, but she still wanted to shower. After all, the Heartbreaker featured live music to dance to as well as temper-soothing beer.

The practical side of her felt certain Jack would be too tired to dance after a day dealing with sick livestock if he had the inclination. She doubted he would. A man who liked to dance wouldn't have gone five and a half years without finding himself even the most casual of partners, which, according to the town gossips, Jack hadn't come close to doing.

She had barely pulled on the new red suede shirt she'd ordered from a catalog and that went great with the black jeans she'd put on when she heard Jack's truck pull up in her driveway.

They were only going for a beer, she stridently reminded herself. Two co-workers sitting in a saloon, rehashing the annoying day they'd had.

A couple of vets who were pretending to be engaged.

She groaned and ran a hand over her frizzy hair. Having caught the look of interest in Jack's eye when he'd first seen her hair down, she'd taken pains to wear it that way each time they went out after work. Granted, she might be setting herself back in her bid to gain the old timers' respect by drawing attention to her femininity, but since the weather had been so bad of late, she figured not many of them would risk the roads for a night on the town.

Thanks to having so little time tonight, she'd been forced to use a hair dryer or risk her wet hair being frozen to her head. So instead of ending up with a head full of tempting locks, she was sporting a mass of frizz. She was about to abandon the whole idea and roll her hair back up into a knot when Jack knocked on the door.

Pete barked and rushed to beat her to the entryway, his three legs still faster than her two. After grabbing her jacket and nudging him out of the way, she opened the door to Jack, who looked up from the toes of his fancy, fine-grained brown boots and greeted her with a heart melting, crooked smile.

He'd showered and changed, too, into a black, western-style shirt and dark denim jeans beneath his dark brown leather coat. Her pulse increased its already rapid pace until her heart smacked against the wall of her chest. Was he hoping to impress her? No, he probably just hadn't wanted to stink like pig wallow longer than necessary.

His eyebrows went up and his smile faltered, and she realized she was scowling. Well, he deserved to be scowled at for looking like every woman's fantasy in denim and leather topped with his sexy smile.

He asked, "Everything okay?" He leaned to the side to look past her into the house. "No problems at Metro Zoo West?"

Pulling on her coat, she answered, "No, everyone's fine." She gave Pete one last pat and gently edged him back so she could slip outside and close the door, using the time it took her to do it to think of an excuse for her expression. "I was just...I was just thinking about what Mr. Webster said when I showed up with you."

"He was paying you a compliment. At least what *he* considers a compliment."

She wrapped her coat closed against the biting cold. "Well I'm not the least complimented by the fact that he thinks I could probably cook as sweet as I look if I stayed home long enough to give it a try."

Jack coughed, doing a poor job of hiding his laughter. "At least he's old enough to think with his stomach and imagine you in the kitchen instead of—"

Her eyes went wide.

"—thinking with..." he trailed off and grinned sheepishly.

Did Jack think with something other than his stomach when he thought about her? The possibility sent her pulse thundering like a flash flood.

He avoided her gaze as he opened the passenger door of his truck, the words Jester Veterinary Clinic painted in black block letters all but obscured by a layer of gravel and mud, and held it for her while she climbed in. She chided herself yet again as he shut the passenger door and went around to the driver's side. The only thing Jack thought with when he thought of her was his brain. Thinking of all the ways his partner "Mel" could help him avoid the likes of Mary Kay and Paula and anyone else who might remind him that he still had a life to lead.

A familiar feeling of inadequacy settled in her stomach.

Jack climbed into the truck and fired up its big engine. Fortunately, the whopping block and a half they had to drive went by too fast to warrant conversation. The weather was too bitter cold to make for a very enjoyable walk, especially after they'd spent most of the day out in it anyway.

They pulled up to the bar and Jack groaned.

"What?"

He gestured toward the plum-colored PT Cruiser. "Paula Pratt."

Melinda sighed in understanding. "She'll be watching us big time."

He grunted, and climbed out of the cab. Melinda followed suit. Jack rounded the cab and halted when he saw her next to the truck.

He threw up his hands with an exasperated noise. "You make it tough for a guy to be a gentleman."

She raised her brows. "Paula's inside." She looked up and down the street. "And no one's around to see, Jack."

He stepped in front of her. "That's not why a man should open a lady's door for her."

"I can open the door myself."

He crossed his arms over his chest. "Among other

things. But I still want to open doors for you. So let me.''

A zing of delight darted through her. Jack was seeing her as a woman. She'd spent her whole life trying to minimize the fact that she was a girl. She would have never imagined being acknowledged as such could give her so much pleasure. But the last thing she wanted Jack to know was how desperate she was for that acknowledgment from him. How pathetic would that be?

She fought a smile and threw up her hands. ''Okay, okay.'' She headed for the swinging doors to the saloon, already feeling the heat rushing out to fight a losing battle with the cold.

Dutifully stepping aside, she allowed him to push one of the old-fashioned doors aside for her. She inadvertently brushed her shoulder against the hard, unchallenged warmth of his chest as she stepped through the doorway and her pleasure turned to a poignant ache. It would be so wonderful to be held against all that heat for real.

Inside the saloon, the Montana cold was firmly held at bay by an effective furnace, a couple dozen bodies heated up by liquor and the amorous hopes it inspired and a whole lot of good old-fashioned hot air. The warmth was a pleasant shock, and Melinda took a moment to let it seep into her, loosening the tightness in her muscles and soothing her tension.

William Devlin, in his late-thirties with short blond hair and blue eyes that made him almost as good-looking as Jack but in a more bad-boy sort of way, greeted them with a knowing grin and salute from his proprietary spot behind the long oak bar. Dev, as he was known, owned the Heartbreaker, and had worked as hard at maintaining the old western ways as Melinda had at breaking them down.

Everything in the large saloon was either scarred, worn oak or polished brass, and highly functional, especially in the case of the spittoons set here and there on the floor. Dev had even managed to find a bartender who looked exactly like a famous country-western singer to help out on busy weekends or when Dev couldn't be around. Roy Gibson, who hailed them as he passed with a trayful of empty beer bottles, was a dead ringer for Willie Nelson, right down to the long, gray braids.

With the Surgeon General's warning considered snake oil by many in these parts, the acrid pall of cigarette smoke floated above the patrons' heads. Melinda was thankful that she was short enough to remain below the worst of the eye-stinging fog.

The band, whose equipment and instruments cluttered the small stage on the far wall, hadn't started their set yet, so the nearby, multicolored jukebox had been employed to make the smoky air throb with country western music.

While she and Jack didn't generate near the stir they first had when they'd started showing up places together, their entrance was still marked by not-so-quick glances and speculative, whispered exchanges. Paula, sitting at the bar with a friend because Bobby Larson had to spend at least some time at home with his wife, did the most amazing job of checking Jack out while at the same time ignoring him.

Melinda hadn't yet grown used to so much attention and reflexively took a step backward. Reaching up to smooth her hair, she was certain she resembled a woolly sheep that had ducked into the bar to escape an overdue shearing.

Jack bumped into her from behind, his big hands grasping her by the waist as if he thought she wasn't sturdy enough to keep her feet. She could feel the strength of his hands through her coat and her temperature soared. She turned her heating face away from the sea of interest and glanced over her shoulder at him. He looked down at her, the glow in his green eyes as reassuring as it was unsettling. He had such a strong physical pull on her without even knowing it.

Then she realized he was amused. Her spine stiffened to bring her back up to her imposing height of five feet four inches and she stepped away from him. He foiled her show of confident independence by snagging her hand as he stepped around her and swaggered further into the saloon. On his way past Dev, Jack held up two fingers, a universal code for two draft beers, and continued to pull Melinda toward an empty table right off the dance floor and show central.

She felt so much more on display than when she'd been cuddled up next to Jack in the movies or at the diner. The Heartbreaker Saloon was a place of sexual ritual, where the males vied for the females through tests of their skill in darts, pool and the fine art of flirting, and the females made their choices according to denim plumage and swaggering preening that most matched their fantasies—at least for that night. Regardless of the basis or the results, the seductions played out here were real, the heady thrill of possibilities and rush of ego-stoked adrenaline shared by both players.

Even knowing she alone would be affected by the sexual atmosphere in their particular twosome, Melinda's pulse and temperature started to climb when the local band scheduled to play that night took to the stage to begin their set. What if Jack wanted to dance? She loved music, but she didn't have much recent experience dancing in the presence of anyone besides her animals. Her cat, One-Eye, wasn't nearly as disconcerting a partner as the tall, masculine, confident male shedding his coat as she was and settling into the chair next to her.

Dev brought over their beers—poured into champagne glasses with cactus stems, no less—himself. "I was wondering how long it would take you two to come in here so I could congratulate you proper with a drink on the house. I was beginning to feel slighted."

Jack made a dismissive noise. "Now Dev, you know that after Melinda and I spend a full day wrestling livestock or tending to black behemoths like your Rufus, we don't have the energy to keep up with the rowdy herd that mills around in here."

Dev scowled in mock indignation. "My cat is not

a behemoth. He's just large and in charge. And you're still young enough to rally, Jack. I'm glad you finally realized that.'' He gave Jack a light punch on the arm. ''But if you need it, I'll have the band play mostly slow songs so you won't be taxed too much.''

The thought of dancing nothing but slow songs with Jack, held close to his big, warm body while they swayed to the music, had Melinda reaching for her beer for a cooling swig.

Dev turned his attention to her and gave a low whistle. ''Melinda, you look great with your hair down that way. I'm kicking myself for not noticing earlier what a catch you are. Promise me you'll come knocking if this joker here doesn't treat you right, okay?''

She knew he was just being nice, but being complimented by a lady-killer like Dev made her cheeks blazing hot. She smiled shyly and dropped her gaze to her beer.

Jack reached over and pulled her chair closer to his. ''In your dreams, Dev. Don't you have a bar to run?''

Dev laughed. ''That I do. Have a good time, you guys, and congrats again.'' He raised a hand in farewell, then went to have a word with the band before going back to the bar.

Melinda glanced at Jack and found him watching her. ''Your hair does look good down. It's gorgeous.'' But he wasn't looking at her hair. His eyes, their green appearing much darker in the muted light, were focused on her eyes, as if he'd made the determination at some earlier date and was only now informing her of it.

She was too unused to compliments to know how to respond when they were delivered lightly, as Dev's had been, let alone when they were given with such seriousness by Jack. She squirmed in her chair a moment, searching for something cleaver or offhand to say in return. She couldn't think of anything, and had to settle for a weak, "Thank you."

"You're welcome," he said in a husky voice. He immediately took a swig of his beer as if to wash whatever was in his throat away, the tall, slender champagne glass looking fragile in his strong hand. He returned the mostly-empty glass to the table and eyed it dubiously. "Sure doesn't hold much, does it?"

"I don't think champagne is supposed to be chugged like beer."

"Would you rather have some champagne? I can have Dev open us some."

"No. No. That's okay. Really," she rushed to reassure him. She was having a hard enough time remembering this wasn't real. "I don't think we have to go that far to convince people."

"That's not why I offered."

Before he could explain further, if he'd intended to, the band's lead singer, a local guy and Garth Brooks wannabe right down to his black-and-white shirt, turned on his mike and called for their attention. Melinda was pretty sure he worked over at the slaughterhouse in Pine Run. He confirmed her suspicion about where he, and undoubtedly his band mates, worked when he introduced the band as The Slaughterhouse Four.

Then he shocked her by saying that there was a newly *outed* couple who deserved a round of applause. "Everybody give it up for Jack and Melinda!" he yelled, whipping off his cowboy hat and pointing at them with it.

The bar, which had been steadily filling up all evening, erupted in hoots and applause. Melinda instinctively covered her face with her hands. Never in her life had she been the object of such positive attention. Though she might have enjoyed it if she and Jack actually were engaged. Because they never would be, Melinda forced herself to lower her hands and soak up the moment despite her discomfort.

When the ruckus died down, the lead singer continued, "And in honor of their engagement, they get to kick off the fun by starting the first slow dance. Get out on that floor, you two."

Melinda's pulse went nuts with the stupidest combination of fear and excitement. She glanced at Jack. He was smiling at the lead singer like a guy with a lot of practice being a good sport. His gaze shifted to her, and he cocked a brow. She probably looked like a thirteen-year-old at her first school dance.

She felt worse. It was as if she'd been stripped bare, her fondest wishes laid out for all to see.

The band started playing a halfway decent cover version of a popular country western ballad and Melinda gripped her hands together in her lap, seized by the urge to dive under the table. Jack, however, pushed his chair back and stood. He offered her his hand, his expression saying, *well, here we go.*

She had no choice. She'd made a deal, after all, and she wanted what she'd be getting out of it—a moment in Jack's arms—more than she wanted to blend into the woodwork. Melinda wiped her damp palm against her jeans then slipped her hand into his. When his warm, strong fingers closed around her hand and he pulled gently to encourage her to stand, her mortification ebbed, replaced by the skittering thrill the prospect of being held close by Jack gave her.

He turned and led her the few steps to the middle of the dance floor, then faced her and brought their joined hands up while he slipped his other one around behind her. She hesitated, but the pressure from his hand on her back encouraged her to step toward him so that they were touching from chest to hip. She slipped her free hand up onto his broad, hard shoulder. He bent his neck and settled his chin just barely against the side of her head. They began to move with the slow, easy rhythm of the song, swaying gently, taking small steps together that felt as natural as if they'd been dancing together all their lives.

She couldn't breathe. But she could feel. Oh, how she could feel. She could feel the strength of his hands. She could feel his heat through his shirt and smell the musky spice of his aftershave. In stark contrast, his belt buckle was cold and hard against her stomach and made her far too aware of what was below that buckle.

And how unaware he was of her.

But then he slid his hand from the middle of her back up under her hair, tangling it in his fingers as he went but doing so without pulling. She could feel him working the strands between his fingers, as if he were enjoying its texture. That small, gentle acknowledgment of her femininity freed the vise that held her chest and she pulled in a deep, blissful breath. Her breasts rose against his chest and he pulled her tighter against him. She wasn't sure, but she thought that perhaps he wasn't so unaware of her, after all.

She could sense an energy building in his body, an attentiveness, perhaps.

She closed her eyes to shut out all the curious faces and rested her head against his chest, focusing on the strong beat of his heart instead of the artificial beat of the music. The strangest sort of peace filled her. Her entire body pulsed with awareness of him, but she'd never felt more calm and sure in her life.

Then it hit her like a flash of summer heat lightning that lit up all the dark corners of her heart she'd foolishly thought she'd known what they held. What she'd felt for Jack when she'd pined for him across the expanse of their desks as he concentrated on paperwork or when she'd surreptitiously watch him run his big hands gently over an animal wasn't love. She'd merely been infatuated with his good looks, incredible body and wounded soul.

She'd been taken with the *idea* of Jack Hartman. A man who needed to be rescued and healed.

But now that she knew what it felt like to be championed by him, personally as well as professionally, and held by him, feeling revered and almost cherished, she realized what being in love with Jack really felt like, what it really meant.

And she realized, really saw, how much it would hurt if he did as he said he would and left town.

Until she was forced to face that day, though, she intended to steal every moment of happiness she could in his arms. With her father, and even Eric, the man she'd thought she'd once loved, she had preferred to go without their affection if she couldn't honestly earn it, which she ultimately never did. With Jack, her monumental pride went by the wayside and she easily turned thief.

To her amazement and delight, they danced the entire set just as they were, fast song or slow, barely acknowledging the congratulations and ribbing doled out in equal measure from those who joined them on the dance floor. When the music finally disappeared, it took a moment for the plain old noise of the crowded bar to bring her back to reality enough to notice that the band had taken a break.

As much as Melinda would have liked to stay in Jack's arms until the jukebox was fired up to keep the good times rolling in the interim, she was forced to step away from him when he straightened and released her. The daydream had come to an end with the jarring sounds of chairs scraping across the scarred floor and the overly bright laughter of women trying desperately to avoid ending the night alone.

Melinda bore her own desperation in silence, as always.

Jack met her gaze briefly before scanning the crowd while running a hand through his thick hair. "It's heating up in here. Would you mind stepping outside for a second?"

An image of them making out up against the building, his big, hot body trapping her against the hard wall, pressing into her, flashed in her mind and her pulse went nuts. "No, not at all," she choked out. "I could use some fresh air." Not to mention a long, deep kiss. She fanned herself with her hand as she followed him to their table to snag their coats and then headed for the door.

Dev looked up from drawing a beer and called, "You aren't calling it a night already, are you? Not that I blame you, though." He winked at them, and the patrons seated at the bar, everyone except Paula and her friend, that is, laughed and nodded knowingly.

When Jack merely shrugged, Melinda felt compelled to explain as she followed him to the swinging doors, "We're just getting some fresh air."

Dev grinned. "Ah. You know, I've heard the air is particularly fresh against the building where the streetlight doesn't reach."

Someone else said, "Heard, nothing, Dev. You've probably tested it yourself."

Another guy added, "Now why would Dev go out

into the cold when he's got a room right there in the back?''

Melinda thankfully stepped through the door Jack held open for her even though the cold air, while it cooled her cheeks, momentarily stole the breath from her lungs. Having her physical relations, pretend though they may be, bantered about by a bunch of bar patrons wasn't something she was comfortable with. Nor did she care to hear about how men like Dev milked every pleasure they could from being single. That sort of daring was as beyond her as city life.

Before they moved away from the light and scant heat escaping from the saloon, Jack helped her into her coat.

''Thanks. So, are we done for the night, after all?'' She dug her gloves out of her pockets and pulled them on.

He remained silent as he put his own coat on and fastened it up. Then he blew out a steamy breath. ''We probably should be. Listen, Melinda, I'm sorry about…about the way I took advantage of the situation in there. It's just been so long since—''

''I'm not sorry, Jack.'' She didn't want to hear him minimize the connection that had been forged between them by blaming it on his lack of physical contact since his wife died. She didn't want him to rationalize away the illusion she'd created for herself. The illusion that he cared for her in the same way she cared for him.

She took a step that closed the distance between

them. She wanted that feeling back. "It was just dancing, Jack. So please, don't say another word."

"But Melinda—"

She yanked off a glove and stopped him by reaching up and placing her fingers on his firm, warm lips. She tapped into the way he'd made her feel on the dance floor to gather the courage to replace her fingers with her lips. She drew away her hand. Focusing on his sensuous mouth, she raised up on her toes.

"Damn it."

Her heart lurched and she jerked back. Dear Lord, what had she done? But Jack wasn't even looking at her. He was scowling at something behind her. She turned and saw the stray dog that Jack and the sheriff had been trying to trap standing not five feet from them, a plastic bag that at one time had held hamburger patties hanging from his mouth. At first glance, his long, gray-tipped coat and slender legs and muzzle did indeed make him resemble a wolf. And his stance was not the least bit submissive, only slightly wary. It was little wonder there were some in town who'd called for the dog to be shot.

She automatically raised a reassuring hand toward the dog and whispered what Jack had obviously already surmised. "We've got to get that plastic away from him before he chokes on it."

His jaw set, Jack slipped his hands into his pockets. "I don't have any treats in this coat. Do you have any on you?"

Melinda put her hands in her pockets but found only tissue and lip balm. "No. I don't."

"I'll have to fake it." He stepped around her and hunkered down to appear less threatening, extending his cupped hand toward the mangy dog.

He took all of two steps, then the dog bolted right past them. Jack lunged for him, but the ground was slick with fresh snow and he fell short, sprawled out on his chest. The dog skirted him easily, almost as if he'd been toying with Jack the entire time. Tail held high, he ran off down the street, his booty still tight in his teeth and flapping in the wind.

"Arrgh," Jack growled, picking himself up off the snowy sidewalk and brushing off.

"You okay?"

"Just pissed. That dog's making me nuts." He brushed his hands off and came back toward her.

He met her gaze and his expression shifted.

Melinda knew in her gut that he was going to go back to what they were talking about before, say something about the way he'd held her when they'd danced. Something that might forever break the tenuous bond they'd made.

Before he could open his mouth, she blurted, "Let's go catch that dog before he chokes to death."

## Chapter Eight

Without giving him time to answer, Melinda took off into the snowy night, running down empty Main Street on the trail of the dog.

"Fool woman," Jack grumbled as he looked dolefully down at his good boots, then at least took the time to grab a length of rope out of the back of his truck and put on his gloves before he lit off after her. That dog didn't want to be caught, and Jack seriously doubted if they'd be able to get close to the animal. He could still see Melinda as she ran straight through the intersection of Main Street and Big Draw Drive, but even if he couldn't see her, her fresh tracks in the snow, directly on top of the dog's prints, were easy enough to follow in the light from the turn-of-the-century streetlamps. Jack's longer legs ate up more ground than Melinda's, but she was still half a block ahead of him when she entered the green glow cast by Jester's lone traffic light hung where Lottery Lane crossed Main Street. She paused for a moment, then canted off to the right, toward Jester Community Park.

Uncertain how the dog would react if she cornered it, Jack increased his speed to catch up with her. He didn't doubt her judgment or skill in handling the dog, and she was somewhat protected by gloves and a heavy coat, but two vets were always better than one when dealing with an unpredictable animal. He finally caught up to her when she stopped beside a tree, her attention on the ground and her breath misting the air around her.

"Lose him?"

She glanced at Jack, a wry grin on her face. She clearly enjoyed the challenge. He'd always assumed she tackled difficult situations with animals more out of dedication, maybe even stubbornness, than anything else, but he realized she found pleasure in solving the problem, doing the job well, also. He liked that.

She gestured to the rope he held coiled in one hand and asked, "You didn't by any chance grab a flashlight, too?"

White Christmas lights had been left up on the library and medical clinic across the street from the park, along with every other business in town. And even though the lights reflected off the snow enough that Jack and Melinda could see their way around, it was by no means light enough to see into the shadows of the trees and bushes scattered around the two-acre park. "No, I didn't. I was too intent on catching up with my crazy partner."

"I'm not crazy. Just maybe a little too enthusiastic." She looked back at the ground and pointed at where the dog's tracks were clear until they reached the base of the bare tree, where they became jumbled with other, older tracks. "The limbs keep the snow from falling as thick here, and there have been other dogs visiting this tree recently." There were several patches of snow at the base of the tree that were definitely yellow.

Jack circled around the tree. "There's not enough light to tell which of these tracks leading away are his."

"Darn dog. I was hoping that chasing him would be enough to spook him into dropping that bag."

"No such luck."

She rounded the tree to stand next to him. "Do you want to keep looking?"

"Yeah. I'd hate for him to choke himself on the plastic." Jack clenched his jaw at the thought of the dog's life ending in such a pitiful way after struggling to survive on his own for so long. He didn't deserve it.

"Then let's keep looking. I worked up enough of a sweat running down here that I'm plenty warm."

"Good." Montana winters didn't lend themselves to nighttime romps outside. "Why don't we spread out a little, so we can cover more ground." He pointed toward the right side of the park. "You swing past the play area in case he went to hide under the play structure, then check out the basketball courts and baseball field. I'll head straight down to the pond and look around there. He might need a drink after being chased by Miss Speedy Vet."

"I did notice that you had a hard time keeping up, old-timer."

He raised the rope. "At least one of us was thinking ahead on the off chance we did catch him. Why don't we meet back up at the pavilion in fifteen minutes. If we haven't spotted him by then, we probably aren't going to, and that's plenty enough time to spend out in this cold."

"Sounds good, Skipper. I'll sound out if I spot him."

"And I'll do the same. Be careful."

"You, too."

They headed off in their prescribed directions. As much as Jack tried to focus on the ground for any sign of fresh tracks from a large dog or a glimpse of said dog beneath the scattered trees and bushes, he couldn't keep from constantly looking in Melinda's direction to make sure she was safe. Which was odd.

For the past six months he'd never once thought about her safety when she went out on calls to the area farms and ranches, often to tend huge, cranky bulls and temperamental hogs weighing hundreds of pounds. Any or all of them could have easily crushed her slight frame against a wall or fence. So why was he suddenly worried about her?

*Because now you know what it feels like to hold her in your arms.* He had no choice but to acknowledge the voice in his head. He couldn't deny it. From the moment he'd held her close and started moving to the music, his way of thinking about Melinda had irrevocably changed. She had ceased to be just an easygoing co-worker he could depend upon. She wasn't even just a funny, caring woman he'd come to know and appreciate better these past weeks.

Melinda was now the woman who made him think about, made him *feel* things he hadn't felt or thought about in five long years.

She was the first woman he'd wanted since Caroline.

The realization hit him in the chest like an unexpected cow kick. He stopped dead in his tracks next to a lump of snow that would be a cluster of cattails in the summer and fall. He wanted Melinda. In self-defense he immediately tried to shake off the significance of it.

He was a healthy guy, after all, and she was a beautiful, sexy woman. He'd just been slow noticing, was all. And since he hadn't known Melinda while Caroline had been alive, there weren't any painful memories connected to her. That's why Melinda was the first to stir sexual feelings in him.

Nodding his head in agreement with his own logic, he started searching for the dog again.

Because the large, open-sided, wooden pavilion, with its gazebolike roof sat near the pond, Jack was the first one there after making a course around the small, frozen body of water. The air, trapped between the peaked roof and the concrete floor, was colder still in the pavilion. Jack's boots sounded sharply against the concrete slab that had been poured to keep the dozen or so picnic tables level and make the pavilion usable during the annual Founders' Day celebration in two weeks.

Only folks in a place like Jester would think nothing of holding an outdoor festival during March in southern Montana.

Jack smiled at the thought. It was little wonder Caroline had loved it here so. She'd been the intrepid sort. The type to build her own picket fence while he'd been at work. Or drive herself to her obstetrician instead of scheduling the appointment when he could have taken her. The scar that day had left on his heart throbbed in a rhythm he'd strangely grown used to. There was something comforting in the pain, much less disturbing than these new stirrings of awareness of Melinda.

As if on cue, Melinda tromped into the pavilion, stomping her feet to knock the snow from her boots. She had the same can-do spirit as Caroline had. Funny how he'd never noticed the similarity before. Although in every other aspect they were completely different.

Caroline had been tall with shoulder-length, straight brown hair and blue eyes. She hadn't been the least bit shy around anyone, whereas Melinda needed time before she allowed her true personality to shine through. And boy, how it shined.

He thought of the excited look on her face as they hunted for the dog's tracks around the tree just a while ago and the fire in her eyes when she railed against the injustice of the Websters' prejudices. Not to mention the funny names she'd given the animals she'd rescued and the love and commitment she showed them. She was like a Montana agate, only showing her beauty to those who took the time to look beneath the surface. But Melinda's surface wasn't so bad, either.

Her hair carried a light dusting of powdery snow, and when she shook it off, flipping her long curls from side to side as she approached him, Jack found himself solidly grounded in the present. When had she become so damn gorgeous?

To redirect his wayward thoughts, he asked, "Any luck?"

She opened one hand and held up a wadded ball of plastic. "Found this, but no dog. Obviously you struck out, too."

"Yep." The reflective glow of the snow didn't penetrate far into the pavilion, so he took the plastic from her hand and examined it as best he could in the gloom. "This is what he had in his mouth, all right, and it doesn't look like he ate any of it. I guess we don't have to worry about him choking tonight."

"Thank heavens. I wasn't exactly in the mood to give a stray dog mouth-to-mouth resuscitation."

Jack's gaze dropped automatically to her full lips and his body pulsed to attention. The image of her mouth covering his, of their breath—and tongues—mingling while mouth to mouth made him instantly hard. There was a growing chemistry between them that he could no longer ignore. "That would have been one lucky dog if you had."

She stilled. "Oh, yeah?"

The hopeful thread in her tone had him shifting toward her. Could it be she felt the attraction, too? Had she been doing more than simply playing along when she molded her body against his on the dance floor? He searched for an answer on her upturned face in the dim light. "Yeah."

Then she licked her lips, and a desire he hadn't felt in five long years roared to life. Though there was no one around to witness it, Jack wanted to kiss her right here, right now, and kiss her damn good.

Without further thought, he leaned down and captured her lips with his. Her mouth was soft and yielding and perfect. When she returned the kiss, sucking his lower lip slightly between her own, the want she'd kindled exploded in his gut and traveled through his veins with white-hot intensity.

He reached up and held her face in his hands, her skin satin smooth and warm to the touch, then deepened the kiss until her mouth opened beneath his. She was so hot and inviting that it seemed the most natural thing to taste her, delving deep with his tongue.

She moaned and swayed against him, gripping his sides, her own tongue meeting his with a seductive stroke. The buzz of pleasure became a roar in his head. He wanted to devour her, to bury himself deep inside her. He thrust his tongue deeper and tilted his pelvis against her, wanting to connect with her, to be inside her everywhere.

*But this is Melinda* a voice from somewhere within the haze of desire reminded him. Definitely no longer Mel, but still a woman he considered a true friend for going along with the charade he'd forced upon her. It wouldn't be fair to her to take their pretend relationship beyond just for show.

Because he still intended to leave the town that she had embraced as her home.

And the town needed a vet.

He eased out of the kiss, exerting all his willpower not to go back for more when she trailed after his mouth with light, eager kisses.

He hadn't realized how hard he was breathing until she rested her forehead against his chest and he felt her head rise and fall. He slipped his hands into her thick hair and held her against him as he struggled for control.

Her voice shaky, she said, "That alone was worth the chase."

Thankful she wasn't upset—by either the liberties he'd taken or the fact that he'd ended the kiss—he chuckled and gently slipped his hands from her hair to release her. He took a step away, not knowing what to say.

Apologizing would be a good place to start. "I shouldn't have done that. I'm sorry."

Her head still bent forward, she whispered, "I'm not."

While she had expressed as much with the way she'd kissed him back, her stating it flat out took him by surprise. "You're not?"

She raised her chin and met his gaze, her brown eyes black and fathomless in the faint light. "No, Jack. I'm not." She slid her hands upward to his chest and flattened her palms over his pecs, making him flex automatically in more than one spot. "No matter what you need, I'm here for you."

Jack couldn't have been more stunned if she'd whipped a fence post out of her pocket and smacked him up side the head. Melinda had just offered herself to him physically as well as emotionally. He couldn't believe he'd thought her simply a good sport. He shook the thought from his head. This meant more. So much more.

Accepting—hell, even acting on—a sexual attraction was one thing, but becoming involved emotionally was taking things too far. He wasn't ready.

And he wasn't staying in Jester.

She gave his chest a light pat then stepped to his side and linked her arm through his. "Come on, let's head back. It's really getting cold." She tugged on his arm and started them walking out of the pavilion.

Bewildered by such a huge shift in their relationship, he let her lead him out of the pavilion and into the ankle-deep, fresh snow on their way back toward Main Street.

"Oh, Jack, your poor boots. I hope you waterproofed them." She gestured down at his feet in a confusing change of subject.

His brain sluggish from his blood having rushed below his belt during their sizzling kiss, he dropped his gaze to his boots. They were covered with snow, but fortunately the ground was frozen solid, so he hadn't sunk into what would have normally been deep mud around the edges of the pond. He absently remarked, ''Considering what I paid for them, I should be able to water ski in them.''

She laughed, a full, rich, throaty sound he'd heard before, but never really thought about. Or reacted to. Just like her breasts, her hair, her lips…

There went that blood again, barreling through his veins, kicking his body to action.

She flashed a quick smile at him that shone bright despite the dim light. ''Too bad the pond's not bigger. I'd like to see that come summer.''

Jack reflexively thought *I won't be here come summer.*

Regret knifed through his chest. Leaving would be that much harder now.

He wasn't shallow enough to believe his attraction to Melinda would simply go away once he was no longer around her. But no matter how tempted he may be at the moment or how much he might continue to want her in the future, he couldn't take up Melinda's offer for that kind of succor. He just couldn't.

She was a woman of worth, and he was a man of honor.

But he'd never been more tempted in his life.

MELINDA SQUEEZED Jack's arm tighter to still the quaking that had begun the second she'd allowed herself to say the words her heart had been screaming.

*No matter what you need, I'm here for you.*

She'd never taken so great a risk in her life. But Jack had handed her such a perfect opportunity to let him know how she felt, at least a little bit, and finish what she'd started outside of The Heartbreaker, that she couldn't allow herself to chicken out. She would have been forever haunted by what-ifs of her own if she had.

And for her trouble he'd kissed her. Lord, how he'd kissed her. It had been the exact kiss she'd longed for after they'd danced.

The dancing had been incredible enough, being held tight in his arms, feeling cherished. But then to have him actually kiss her—Melinda could have died right then and there a very happy woman.

Only now what?

How could she carry on as they had before, sitting across their desks from each other with the taste of him imprinted on her brain, the feel of his hands in her hair etched forever in her heart?

The same way she dealt with everything difficult in her life, like knowing her father had wanted a boy instead of her and that the old timers in Jester didn't think she could do the job—by gritting her teeth and doing what she needed to do. Hopefully Jack wouldn't make a big deal out of her offer.

She didn't hold out much hope that he would actually let her take care of *all* of his needs. His reluctance to begin his life anew ran too deep.

She risked a quick glance up at his face. His strong jaw still looked a little slack, though he didn't have quite the deer-in-headlights expression that he'd had after she'd told him she wasn't sorry they'd kissed. He hadn't run screaming for the hills, though. She took that as a good sign. Just maybe he'd let her heal him yet.

As they walked back up Main Street, the sounds of alcohol-induced laughter and loud conversations from those who'd needed to cool off or sober up outside of the saloon reached them.

Uncertain about how Jack might behave if they went back in, and unwilling to find out in front of a crowd of people, she said, "We're still going to call it a night, right?"

The last thing Melinda wanted to do was try to figure out if any attention he gave her during the course of the rest of the night was because of what had happened between them or simply to satisfy an audience. After experiencing a taste—literally—of Jack's affection, she needed to be as clear as she could be about his motivation from here on out for her sanity's sake.

He looked at her for a moment before answering. "Probably should."

They were spotted by the small cluster of bar patrons and loudly hailed. She and Jack had to endure all sorts of bawdy speculation about what they'd been up to, most of it animal mating rituals related, as he opened his truck's passenger door for her then rounded the vehicle and climbed in himself. Melinda took Jack's lead and merely smiled and waved in response.

As Jack started up the engine, Melinda blew out a steamy breath. "Jeez, are they starved for entertainment, or what?"

"I think it's more the novelty of the town's vets being involved with each other."

More hopeful that they might actually become involved for real than she'd ever thought she'd be, she pulled in a bracing lungful of cold air and tried her best to sound causal. "Whatever."

She was about to risk thanking Jack for the evening when she noticed him looking at the snow shrouded statue on the Town Hall lawn directly in front of them as he made the left turn from Main Street to Mega-Bucks Boulevard.

The statue that he had said reminded him of his late wife every time he passed it.

Melinda's heart twisted. He was right. Jester was a town full of memories. But could they possible make enough new ones for themselves to ease the pain of his loss? Only Jack could answer that. And Melinda was too afraid to ask the question. She wasn't certain she could handle the answer.

The blasting heater had barely made a dent in the frost on the windshield before Jack was pulling into her driveway, the snow crunching beneath the wheels. She made a point to comply with his previous request and sat tight until he could get out and walk around the truck to open her door for her, but her compliance didn't seem to register with him as he opened the passenger door. Had the reminder of his wife made him regret what had happened between them? The prospect made her bleed.

He walked with her to the house, but stayed on the bottom concrete step when she took the next step up onto the little front porch, like he wanted to keep his distance from her. Heaven help her if he regretted what had happened between them tonight. She pulled her house key out of her pocket and unlocked the door.

With a hand on the knob and a lump the size of a boulder in her throat, she turned and forced out, "Thank you, Jack, for tonight."

Though his green eyes were on a level with hers as he met her gaze, his thoughts were still unreadable despite the stark light from the ugly bare bulb she needed to buy a cover for next to the door. She prayed her expression was just as enigmatic, that he couldn't see how desperately she wanted to wrap her arms around him and never let go.

Because no matter how badly she might want him, she didn't want him to come to her out of pity.

He tilted his head to the side and raised a hand, skimming her cheek with the back of his fingers, and she knew she'd failed to hide her emotions. God, how he must feel sorry for her.

He surprised her by leaning forward and catching her lips with his in a quick, sweet kiss. Then he pulled back and said, "You're welcome." His baritone was deeper than usual, sounding as though the words were coming from deep within him.

But he still turned and walked away from her toward his truck, taking her shredded heart with him.

## Chapter Nine

Jack sat alone in a booth at The Brimming Cup, staring into his third cup of coffee that morning and trying to come to terms with what had happened between him and Melinda the night before. He'd had plenty of time to think about their kiss this morning because his schedule of Saturday office appointments had dropped off considerably since word of his and Melinda's engagement had made it around town. It was amazing how Mary Kay's cat, Pumpkin and Paula's little dog, Killer—make that *Angel*—had suddenly become healthy again. Making himself ineligible had worked better than he'd hoped in getting the gold diggers to leave him alone.

Time to think didn't always lead to a solution, or understanding, though. He'd only managed to think himself into one circle after another the same way an unsettled horse will walk the fence of its corral, searching for the way out.

He knew he shouldn't take his pretend relationship with Melinda into the realm of reality because it wasn't fair to her; he still intended to leave. But he wanted her. His wanting her brought on a hefty dose of guilt, which made him think of Caroline, which reminded him of why he needed to leave. This town had been Caroline's and as long as he stayed here, he'd never feel free to move on with his life.

Not even with Melinda.

He swirled the cup, making the coffee go round and round to match his thoughts.

"Jack." Luke's voice brought his head up. He hadn't noticed the sheriff approach, let alone the fact that he was standing at Jack's table still in his suede, sheepskin lined coat and tapping his Stetson against his jean-clad leg. Luke's blue eyes were clouded with uncharacteristic emotion that looked remarkably like grief.

Apprehension stabbed Jack in the chest. "What is it?"

Luke ran a tanned hand through his short, jet-black hair. "It's Henry. When he didn't show up for their Saturday morning breakfast bull session or answer his phone, Finn called me and asked me to go out to Henry's place. I did, and I found him. He'd passed away in his sleep sometime last night, Jack."

A horribly familiar disbelief grabbed Jack by the throat. *"He's dead?"*

"I'm afraid so. The coroner and Doc Perkins are already on their way out, but I figured I should come get you. Finn's gonna need some help finding Henry's papers, and well, just dealing with everything. We all know Henry would want you to be the one to help Finn out."

Jack sat back as shock warred with old companions of his, the indignation of loss and terrible, terrible grief. "I knew he'd been tired lately—hell, for the last ten years—but I had no idea his health was that bad."

"He hadn't taken care of himself since Dolly died, Jack, you know that."

Jack did know it. All too well. Like Jack, Henry had fallen victim to fate's cruelty.

He slammed a hand down on the table. "Damn it. I should have done something about it."

"Henry chose his own path, Jack. There was nothing any of us could have done."

Unswayed by Luke's reasoning, Jack shoved himself from the booth and stood. "My truck's down the way. I'll follow you out to Henry's."

Taking refuge in the practical, he focused on the fact that on the way he'd have to call Melinda to come in and cover his appointments, or reschedule them if she had some of her own. He paid for the breakfast that had come with his first cup of coffee while Luke quietly filled Shelly in on the reason for their ashen appearances and somber moods.

"Henry Faulkner passed away last night."

Shelly's eyes went wide and she covered her mouth with her hand. "Oh, no." She dropped her hand. "How? What happened?"

With a half shrug, Luke said, "Nathan is on his way out to Cottonwood Farm right now. But it looked to me like he died in his sleep. He looked real peaceful."

Her eyes welled with tears. "He'll be so missed."

Luke nodded in agreement. "That he will."

She turned her big, glittering hazel eyes to Jack. "I'm so sorry, Jack."

Jack's throat was too tight to respond. He raised an acknowledging hand and left the diner.

As Jack strode down the sidewalk toward where he'd parked his truck in front of the vet clinic, an icy numbness crept under his skin that had nothing to do with the freezing air or the flat gray sky that threatened yet more snow. It was kin to the numbness that had seen him through the days after Caroline's funeral. He didn't particularly remember much about the days before.

Cell phone reception was notoriously bad in Jester, so he went in to use the clinic phone to call Melinda with the news. Her soft voice and gentle understanding nearly undid him.

But he forced himself to think of nothing save getting in his truck and following behind Luke's dark, sheriff department SUV as he drove out to the Faulkner farm ten miles northeast of town. He refused to think about how much he would miss Henry's understanding gaze when Jack dropped his sorry rump next to Henry, Finn and Dean inside the barbershop and watched the world that was Jester go by while Dean and Finn provided the color commentary. Henry had had nothing but time since he'd sold Faulkner Hardware and retired. Finn, the retired town librarian, was also a widower, but had a big family to keep him happy. And Dean knew everything about everyone, whether they came into his barbershop or not.

Jack wouldn't think about those times. He couldn't.

The numbness was fully in place by the time he passed the farm Luke and his sister Vicki had grown up on, but their parents had since sold, then turned into the pothole riddled drive leading to Cottonwood Farm. When he reached Henry's farmhouse with its peeling paint and air of neglect, surrounded by gigantic maple trees that looked equally forlorn without their leaves, Jack pulled in off to the side beneath one of the trees so he wouldn't block in Luke, Doc Perkins, whose rig was already there, or the coroner when he arrived. Jack had a feeling he was going to be here a while. It took time to close the book on a person's life.

He stepped up onto the porch and walked through the open front door and realized that in the eight years Jack had known him, Henry had never invited him into his house. Jack had been to the farm plenty of times to treat Henry's animals before he sold them off, but they had always gone straight to the barn and stayed there.

Jack stepped into the house, lit by the eerie gray morning light coming through windows Jack distinctly remembered as always being blocked by the heavy curtains that were now thrown wide. He looked around and realized why he'd never been invited in.

Henry had not only ceased to take care of himself after Dolly died, he'd let his house go to hell in a newspaper and garbage stuffed handbag, too. Everywhere he looked there was trash of some sort. And where there wasn't yellowed newspapers or discarded mail, there were reminders of Dolly.

Her reading glasses occupied the only uncluttered spot on a little table next to a once-comfortable looking chair. Her knitting was in a basket on the floor in front of the chair, as if she'd just set it down to go tend to something else.

Henry had clearly not taken Dolly's death well. And that had occurred ten years ago.

Jack was too stunned to process it all.

Tall, lanky Finn, wearing dark blue slacks and a white oxford shirt, came out of the kitchen. His thick white hair was unusually mussed, eyes red-rimmed behind his wire frame glasses and he was blowing his nose into a paper napkin. "Hell of a day to forget my handkerchief."

The frost under Jack's skin began to melt, and his own eyes started to burn. With the return of his grief came his anger. Why hadn't Henry let anyone help him?

Finn blew his nose again.

Knowing all too well that there was nothing more he could say, Jack offered, "I'm sorry, Finn."

"So am I, Jack. So am I. But that stupid old geezer was just waiting to die, you know. Never did want to go on without his Dolly, no matter how hard Dean and I tried to convince him otherwise." He moved to the foot of the stairs where Luke could be heard talking to Doc, their words indistinct.

The sound of a car pulling up reached them. Jack

leaned toward a window. "County coroner is here. I'm going to go up and…and say goodbye." Something he hadn't been able to do with Caroline. They'd said the damage she'd sustained in the wreck was too great, and they wouldn't let him see her.

Finn nodded and waved the napkin at the stairs. "Yes. Good. Go."

Jack followed the sound of Luke and Doc's voices to find the right bedroom. The two other men were standing in what looked like a study at the end of the hall, though, on either side of a little cot. Henry was laid out on it flat on his back, head propped up slightly by a pillow and his hands folded neatly over his chest atop the white-and-peach quilt bedding. Despite the wild, sparse gray hair sticking out on either side of his head, Henry had never looked so peaceful.

Some of Jack's anger dissipated. Henry was finally where he'd wanted to be—with his beloved Dolly.

Jack glanced at Dr. Nathan Perkins. Doc was only three years older and a couple of inches shorter than Jack, but his prematurely grayed hair gave him a distinguished, mature air that fit his role in town. He was no longer the only doctor around since he'd brought in Shelly's new husband, Connor O'Rourke, to help at the medical clinic Doc had been upgrading with his share of the lottery, but he was still considered Doc.

Gesturing at Henry, Jack asked, "Is that how…?"

Doc raised a hand in greeting. "Hey, Jack. Yep, that's exactly how Luke found him. Like the old guy had simply laid down to die. But he probably went in his sleep. It happens," he explained gently, closing up the black medical bag on the cluttered desk with an ominous snap.

Jack nodded, fighting the swell of devastating pain in his throat, wanting the blessed numbness back. Looking around at the study, with Henry's clothes piled in the corners, Jack was momentarily distracted. "Was he using this as his bedroom?"

Blowing out a heavy breath, Doc said, "Appears so."

Jack feared he knew why.

Luke strode toward him. "We'll give you a minute."

Doc moved toward the door also. "Yes, of course. Was that the coroner I heard drive up?"

Jack nodded, his gaze on the serene-looking old man on the cot.

"Good."

They both stepped around Jack. Luke, who Henry had been real fond of, also, paused long enough to place an understanding hand on Jack's shoulder before leaving the room.

Jack moved slowly to Henry's side. Even though there had been so much Jack hadn't known about Henry, he'd been a good friend. He would sorely miss the cranky old bird's unique understanding of Jack's pain.

He selfishly wanted Henry back, though not with the consuming, burning need that had damn near crippled him after Caroline's car crash. But he'd laid Caroline and the child she would forever hold beneath her heart to rest. He truly had. The ache was bearable now. He dealt with death often enough to be forced to accept it as a part of life, no matter how brutally unfair.

It was just such a risk to care.

No matter how much Jack wanted to change what had happened here, too, there was no denying the peaceful smoothness Henry's once-lined face had settled into.

A calming acceptance seeped into the wounds in Jack's heart. "I suppose you're finally happy now. That's good. I guess this was the only way you'd get that. God bless your soul, Henry. Rest in peace old friend."

Jack turned and headed back downstairs, his jaw clenched tight against the swell of sadness threatening to crest in his chest.

Finn stepped away from the knot of men standing near the front door. "Jack, do you have time to spare today? There are some things that need to be seen to right away, like what little Henry had in the fridge and the cupboards, draining the pipes so they don't freeze, as well as finding where he stuck his important papers. Apparently anything that didn't have to do with Dolly got put God knows where."

"Of course." Jack glanced between Finn and Luke. "The only kin he has left is his granddaughter, right? Has she been notified?"

They both shook their heads.

Finn said, "Don't know where Jennifer is. She stopped coming to visit after Dolly passed on. Hopefully Henry has her number somewhere, but I honestly don't know if he kept in contact with her. He probably hid it if he did have it. You know how paranoid he'd been getting as of late.''

Finn let out a heavy sigh as he surveyed the living room. "I tell you, Jack, this is one job I don't look forward to. I had no idea he'd gotten this bad."

While the coroner, Doc and Luke saw to taking Henry's body to the funeral home in Pine Run and starting the necessary paperwork, Jack and Finn went to work on the house. The first order of business, after the garbage was cleared away, that is, was finding Henry's will, if he had one. He should have had one because all of the lottery winners had been advised to have that sort of documentation put in order ASAP.

By late afternoon they still hadn't found any sign of a will, but they had unearthed what they hoped was Jennifer Faulkner's address. Luke would be able to come up with a phone number from it and could contact her. The thought of a young woman, though she probably wasn't much younger than Jack, soon being told that she no longer had any blood relatives—Finn had told him how she'd lost her parents in a plane crash—dissolved Jack's protective numbness completely. It was one thing to be separated from family by distance, but to be left alone by death was tough.

As the early winter darkness descended on the late Henry Faulkner's farm, the ache Jack had been fighting clawed its way out of his heart and settled dead center in his chest with breath-stealing intensity when he walked into a room upstairs that turned out to be the master bedroom with a big four-poster bed. It was the only room in the house that had been kept clean and neat. And it looked as if Dolly had only just been there. A half-full glass of water sat on the nightstand. A pair of women's slippers were tucked beneath the edge of the bed and a pink robe was laid out on the coverlet.

It was as if Henry had hoped she would soon return.

Jack's earlier intuition regarding Henry's sleeping arrangements proved true.

Henry's words when he'd congratulated Jack and Melinda kept coming back to him over and over again.

*You're too young to end up like me, Jack.*

It made sense now. Henry hadn't wanted Jack to end up like this, living in the past, waiting to die.

Jack thought of his own house as he cleaned out the perishable contents of Henry's. While his house wasn't a mess—and unlike Henry, Jack had boxed up his wife's clothes and other non-keepsake items and donated them to charity—he hadn't changed much of anything in the past five years. Though it certainly hadn't been a conscious choice. Not really. It was just easier to leave things as they were.

Easier and less painful. But he was only thirty-three years old. And he did not want to end up like Henry. Jack still had a hell of a lot of life yet to live.

A life he could spend at least a little of in the comforting arms of a woman like Melinda Woods.

AFTER THE EMOTIONAL HELL of the day, Jack was operating on autopilot as he drove away from Henry's that night, so he wasn't entirely surprised when he realized he'd driven straight to Melinda's little house. He wasn't all the way out of his truck yet when the front door opened and she came out into the cold to meet him. She must not have been home long because she was wearing the red flannel shirt that looked so good with her blond hair and snug jeans she often wore to work. And her hair was still tied up in some sort of knot behind her head.

Part of him wished she were wearing her silky pajamas with her hair hanging wet down her back. But the rest of him was just plain damn glad to see her. Her big brown, soft eyes were shiny in the porch light, her empathy for his loss right out there on her sleeve.

She immediately grabbed his hand, her small palm warm and comforting against his. "Oh, Jack. I'm so sorry about Henry. How awful. Have you been out there all day?"

He nodded as he continued toward the front door, his throat suddenly too tight to speak.

"Oh, boy. I was afraid of that." She went through the door first, holding an exuberant Pete at bay until Jack could come in and close the door behind him. "And you probably haven't eaten anything at all, either. I have some soup all ready to go. I came home earlier in the day and got it going. I was about to take it over to your place so it would be there for you when you got home because I...I wasn't sure if I'd see you.''

His chest burned with emotions stirred up by the day, and Jack didn't waste another second. He instinctively reached for Melinda, snagged her around the waist and pulled her against him. Wrapping his arms around her, he hugged her for all he was worth, holding her warmth, her softness, as tight against him as he could.

He buried his nose in her hair to breathe in deep her comforting citrus smell, only tonight it was muted by the earthy smell of the outdoors and a hint of the disinfecting soap they used after treating an animal.

She squeaked and the toes of her boots bumped against his shins. Only then did he realize he'd picked her clean up off the ground and was probably crushing her. He eased his hold and let her slip down the front of him until she was back on her feet. The friction created by her soft curves rubbing along the length of him made him want to groan and snatch her right back up again.

He met her wide-eyed gaze. ''I didn't mean to crush you.''

She smiled gently and reached a hand up to his whiskered jaw. ''Jack, you can crush me anytime.''

*No matter what you need, I'm here for you.*

Her words from the night before in the pavilion hung unspoken between them. He searched her gaze, wondering if he should risk taking what he truly needed from her. Did he dare get that close to another human being again?

She broke the spell by stepping away from him with a deep sigh. "You should eat, though. Come on." She snagged his hand again and led him to the little oak table in the kitchen nook. "Sit down and let me take care of you."

Jack eased himself into the wooden chair facing the kitchen, his chest tightening. It had been a long time since anyone had taken care of him. Maybe that was all he needed from her. A little comforting, a little nurturing, a little care.

As Melinda laid out a place setting in front of him, something rubbed against his leg. He looked down to find her big white cat, Mr. Booger, bumping his fat cheek against Jack's shin, then arching his back and rubbing his side along Jack's jeans. The cat left a trail of white hair in his wake.

Jack sought out the rest of her animals with his gaze. If anyone could handle taking care of the likes of him, Melinda could. He looked back at her as she poured chunky, steaming, heavenly smelling soup from a large, wide-mouth thermos into a bowl. She'd caught her tempting bottom lip in her teeth as she concentrated. Her full breasts no longer missed his notice beneath her shirt and her rounded bottom was incredibly enticing in her jeans as she stood with one hip out.

Jack's body responded instantly with heat and hardness.

The burn of sexual need knocked aside the searing pain of loss in Jack's gut and he accepted the fact that he wanted a hell of a lot more from Melinda than a bowl of warm soup.

He shifted in his chair and watched her carry the brimming bowl of soup over to him, concentrating on not spilling as she came to stand next to him. She didn't meet his gaze until she'd set the bowl on the plate in front of him. Some of what he was feeling must have shown in his expression because her tawny eyebrows twitched upward and she paused, hands extended.

Jack took advantage of her surprise, shock, whatever and put a hand on the back of her toned thigh, sliding it upward over her delectable, firm bottom, which he resisted the urge to squeeze because he'd been raised a gentleman, until he reached the dip in her waist just above her hipbone. It was his favorite spot on a woman, and he couldn't believe how alive it made him feel to touch her there.

He closed his eyes and pulled in a deep breath, his head filling with the savory smell of the soup and the dizzying prospect of rejoining the living, then let it out with a "Mmm" before opening his eyes again.

Melinda shifted, first toward him, then away slightly. "Ah...it's, ah, it's vegetable beef soup."

He gave her waist a gentle squeeze. "Feels like gorgeous woman to me."

She made a choking sound that was half cough, half gasp. "Are you okay, Jack?"

He opened his eyes and looked up at her. Her pretty brown eyes were wide and her cheeks flushed to the same red as her flannel shirt. "Yeah, I am. I really am."

With a slow movement she eased away from him, slipping into the chair on his right. He couldn't help moving his leg so that his knee rested against hers. Heat spread from the point of contact upward.

"I know how much Henry meant to you, Jack. That having to face another…that losing him so suddenly is hard to bear."

The pain squashed beneath his newly awakened attraction to Melinda twitched at her condolences, but now that he was here, now that he'd decided to reclaim at least a small measure of his life, he refused to let it up again.

The smell of the soup conspiring with his stomach finally convinced his brain that he did need to eat. He shook his head and picked up the spoon. "It was what Henry wanted. I never realized how badly until I saw the inside of his house for the first time today."

"You'd never been before?"

He took a spoonful of the soup, closing his eyes for a moment in satisfaction that the rich broth and tender meat tasted as good as it smelled. It was as if allowing himself to be attracted to Melinda had ratcheted up his other sensations as well.

After swallowing, he said, "No, I hadn't. Had never been invited in. Now I know why." He took another bite, enjoying the flavors.

Melinda sat forward with her brows high. "And?"

"Henry had set up damn near a shrine to his late

wife, Dolly, who passed away ten years ago. You wouldn't believe it, Melinda.''

She sat back and dropped her gaze to her hands in her lap. "Oh, I don't know about that.''

He shot her a glance. "What do you mean?''

She shrugged. "Nothing.'' A long curl escaped her knot, dropping onto her breast like a thick strand of honey. She met his gaze again. "Is that what he did with his lottery winnings?''

His train of thought lost in the urge to undo the rest of her hair and bury his hands in it, he didn't answer for a moment. Forcing himself to focus, he said, "From what I could tell, Henry didn't do a single thing with his share. Except maybe buy newspapers. There were a lot of newspapers. And he never got rid of a single one. Everything else was exactly the way it had been ten years ago.''

She shrugged again. "From what I can tell, all you've bought are those fancy cowboy boots you had on the other night.''

He thought of his boots sitting next to his back door drying, and pushed aside the uncomfortable twinge her words caused. "You know what I'm saving my money for.''

She considered her hands again, her luscious mouth slightly downturned. "Yes, I do.''

Her soft voice pulled Jack toward her. He leaned forward and snagged the curl from where it clung to her flannel shirt above her breast. "At least I have a plan for the future, Melinda. I'm not stuck in the past.''

She looked at him, her brown eyes as rich as sable beneath a sheen of moisture. "Are you sure, Jack?"

A spasm gripped his heart and he placed a hand against her warm, satiny cheek, his thumb stroking her cheekbone with the lightest touch he was capable of. "I am now," he murmured, then he kissed her.

## Chapter Ten

Her heart soaring, Melinda opened her mouth beneath Jack's and allowed him to deepen the kiss. He tasted of savory soup, man and sorrow. A sorrow she could at least provide a balm for, if not heal. She wanted to show Jack he wasn't alone in this world; he didn't have to bear the weight of his loss like a single scrub pine heaped with heavy snow out in the middle of nowhere.

She reached up and wrapped her arms around the back of his neck, praying with everything she was worth that he understood her message. He slanted his head to better fit his mouth against hers and her entire body wanted to be there to meet the tip of his tongue when he thrust it into her mouth. It connected with hers, and she felt like she'd grabbed hold of a wire fence electrified with pleasure.

He slid his hand from her cheek into her hair and splayed his fingers across her scalp, kneading and holding her while he made love to her mouth with his. His other hand slipped beneath her arm and held her side, just off her breast, tempting her to turn into his touch. The simmering desire she'd always carried for him rolled to a full boil, creating a pressure inside her chest she had no choice but to relieve with a moan.

As if she'd given him a signal, he abruptly dropped his hand from her side and grabbed a leg of her chair, jerking her closer to him with the loud scraping noise of wood on linoleum.

Against his mouth she said, "Good thing I bought a round table instead of a square one with dangerous corners."

With a half chuckle, half growl that reverberated around in his chest and spurred something very instinctual deep inside of her, he said, "But you're still not close enough."

She was darn near giddy with a resounding need. "Tell me about it."

He kissed her again, hot and teasing. Without ending the kiss, he took his hand from her hair and found the backs of her knees with both hands. Before she realized what he meant to do, he yanked her off her chair and into his lap, her legs straddling his lean hips. The heat and hardness she came in contact with made her gasp. He took advantage of it and kissed her deeply.

His big, capable hands went between them to her breasts, cupping, kneading and stroking them through her clothes with just enough pressure to make her ache for more. She reminded herself that they weren't teenagers making out in a car or college students fumbling through a hasty, almost perfunctory introduction to adulthood. They were two people who'd been alone for far, far too long, who deserved this sort of connection, who had every right to take it all the way.

Made bold by his desire, Melinda took her arms from around his neck and reached over his hands to find the buttons on her shirt. Bold or not, her fingers still shook as she unbuttoned her shirt, yanking it from beneath the waist of her jeans so she could unfasten it completely.

Jack rumbled his approval and broke away from her mouth to kiss his way down the path she was creating. Melinda dropped her head back and lost herself to the ripples of incredibly wonderful sensations his moist, warm mouth created on her skin. When his lips reached the lacy edge of her white demi bra, he darted his tongue beneath the fabric and sent a bolt of sizzling pleasure straight to her womb.

She groaned his name, and he responded by opening her shirt wider, then unerringly found the front clasp between her breasts and opened her bra. Vulnerability lanced through her when the cool air contacted her overheated flesh, making her skin tighten. She dropped her chin to watch him.

The kitchen light glinted off where the sun had kissed his thick, light brown hair and his strong, square jaw, shadowed by emerging whiskers, was set as he focused his attention on what he was doing. His touch featherlight and his gaze hot and heavy, he pushed the undergarment to the sides. With near reverence he placed a hand beneath each breast.

His voice thick and rough edged, he whispered, "How could I have been so blind?"

Before she could think of a suitable response, one that wouldn't remind him of his pain, he dipped his head and took the puckered tip of her right breast into his mouth. Any thought not directly related to the way her breast felt trapped between his lips as his hot, moist tongue rolled around her nipple evaporated from her mind. She let her head drop backward again.

He lavished her breast with attention until every bone in her body felt soft and ready for him to shape her around him like the most pliant of clay. Replacing his mouth with his fingers, he kissed his way to her other breast and rewarded it with equal attention.

The passion he'd so casually thrown a match to flared suddenly and raced through her like a wildfire across tinder-dry plains. She arched toward him, into his kiss, rocking forward against the hard ridge beneath her. He growled and raised his head from her breast and found her mouth again.

He gripped her hips, encouraging her to ride him, but it was too much, the sensation was too intense. She broke the kiss and bowed away from him, her heart thundering in her ears.

Resting her forehead against his, she breathlessly said, "Ah, Jack. You're killing me here."

"I think that's suppose to be my line." He bucked against her slightly as if she could have missed how turned on he was.

She automatically ground down on him and made him groan.

His expression intense, an undeniable need darkening his field-green eyes, he reached up a hand to cup her cheek again. "I want to be inside of you, Melinda."

Her breathing hitched as every muscle in her pelvis clenched in anticipation, but despite her body's response to the potential reality of his words, her brain stuck on the noticeable fact he hadn't used the words *make love.* But how could she expect that from Jack? Loving had cost him so much once. She doubted he'd ever want to risk having to experience that sort of pain again.

Her body didn't give a damn and overruled her mind, caring only that he wanted to be a part of her.

Between shallow breaths she said, "Okay."

He pulled back to meet her gaze, his pupils dilated by desire, providing her a way inside of him in return. He raised a playful brow. "Just *okay?*"

"Yep. I'm a woman of few words, Jack. Action is loads better." She rocked against him again and was rewarded by him closing his eyes in obvious pleasure.

"Mmm. When you're right, you're right, darlin'," he drawled. He shifted his big, hot hands to cup her bottom. "Come on. Let's go do some living."

The muscles in his legs flexed and he stood in one fluid motion, his chair thunking against the wall as he pushed it back.

"Oh!" Melinda reflexively tightened her hold on his neck and wrapped her legs around his waist, but it was clear he could easily carry her without her help.

A part of her was unable to fully accept that what

was about to happen was really going to happen. The part of her Eric had beaten down by choosing another, "better" woman made it hard for her to believe that a man as desirable as Jack could want her. And she had fantasized so often of making love with Jack that to have it actually happen made her feel incredibly awkward.

He headed toward the short hall off the living room. "I'm assuming your bedroom's down here?"

"The door on your left. Bathroom's on the right."

But rather than watching where he was going, his gaze dropped to her bared breasts again. It had been so long since she'd shared any sort of intimacy with a man, a ridiculous sort of shyness had her searching for a way to distract him.

She teased, "You know, your soup is going to get cold."

"I'm hungry for something else, sweetheart. Starving, in fact." He captured her lips and proceeded to walk them into the living room wall, having missed the opening to the hall.

Though far too sensitized by what was going on with her front side to give a darn about what happened to her backside, she was surprised enough to let out a grunt.

He tried to pull away from their kiss, but she wouldn't let him, so he murmured against her lips, "Sorry."

She giggled, sucked at his bottom lip, then pulled away enough to say, "No problem. I just hope you have better aim with other things."

His grin was wicked. ''Hey, I happen to know all sorts of things about mating.''

A delicious shiver of delight and anticipation wracked her, and she buried her face against his neck as he readjusted his course and went down the hall. She couldn't believe this was actually happening.

A dark voice reminded her of the reasons why he was doing this, that he'd been hurting and needed a distraction to get through it. And that he'd said nothing to suggest he'd changed his mind about leaving.

She refused to care. She wanted this memory, this moment with Jack. She'd deal with the baggage later. She proved her point to herself by lifting her head and kissing him for all she was worth.

He paused and made that rumbling sound deep in his chest again. Using his shoulder along the wall to find the door opening, he turned into her darkened bedroom, a place she'd thought he'd never see. He didn't end the kiss until he'd laid her gently on the queen-size bed.

He straightened and looked around the small room. Melinda cringed, knowing what he saw in what light from the kitchen that made it into the room. While she wasn't a slob, she wasn't exactly a neatnick, either. The batch of dark laundry she'd washed two days ago still sat where she'd dumped it in the room's lone chair—a cute, skirted, overstuffed chair upholstered in white-and-rose checked chintz. She'd bought it thinking she'd use it to sit and read in or at the very least use to put her shoes on. It was always too buried beneath laundry, clean or not, to do either, so much so even the cats wouldn't risk jumping up on the teetering pile.

Jack returned his gaze to her, the green of his eyes darkened and intense. "You are so much more than I'd first thought you were."

She resisted the urge to close the front of her shirt. "How so?"

"I hadn't expected such…femininity."

Though she knew what he meant, she raised her brows and glanced down at her exposed chest.

A corner of his mouth kicked up and he put a knee on the bed and climbed on next to her. "Not that, so much as girly-ness."

Jack seeing her as feminine unsettled her. When she was ten, her dad had finally put to words his dearest wish that she'd been born a boy. She'd finally understood why he would look at her, his mouth tight and downturned, then walk away. Since then, Melinda had shunned the trappings of femininity in an attempt to win his love. And it hadn't worked.

She glanced toward the padded headboard she'd covered with the same rose and cream fabric she'd made the duvet cover from. The material had been on sale. She used the mound of crochet-edged pillows she'd made during a stretch of long, lonely nights to prop herself up with while she read veterinarian journals in bed.

Above the bed hung a wreath of dried lavender her mother had made her as a housewarming gift when Melinda had first moved to Jester. Mom had picked the lavender from a plant that grew outside the kitchen door, and it reminded Melinda of her child-hood home.

Each and every touch in this room had sprung from a practical or sentimental reason. But was that why she'd failed to win her father's love? Because she'd failed to minimize the fact she was a girl? Or did it go deeper than that?

Jack took her mind from her thoughts when he dropped his head and starting kissing his way down her neck, following the same path with his mouth that he'd taken in the kitchen. He kissed and licked his way to her left breast, then took her hardened nipple between his lips and sucked. Suddenly not giving a damn what anyone but Jack thought, Melinda was exceedingly glad to be a woman.

His tongue played at the sensitive tip and she arched toward him as if he'd winched her tight. An urgency overtook her, and Jack seemed to sense it. He quickly stripped her clothes from her, kissing every new patch of exposed skin. Whenever she could, she unbuttoned and tugged off what she could reach of his clothes. What she uncovered made her heart pound.

She'd known he was in excellent shape, having seen him in action hauling an unwilling cow into the chute for vaccinations or lifting a full-grown sheep over a fence. But a show of strength or even the hint of rounded muscle beneath his clothing didn't prepare her for the male beauty of Jack's naked body. Every muscle was perfectly delineated without being too bulky. His broad chest had just enough hair spread across it to tempt her to tangle her fingers in it.

She reached for him, and his touch and kisses took on a similar air of urgency.

"Ah, Melinda, Melinda," he murmured against the base of her throat as he settled his big, muscular, hot body on top of her. Melinda understood. Despite his teasing, despite his seemingly casual air, Jack desperately needed this. He needed to be reminded that he was still very much alive. Alive, and for this moment in time, entirely hers.

"Make love to me, Jack."

He kissed her hard and deep and covered her with his incredible body, bringing every inch of her skin to life. But before she could wrap her arms around him and open her legs to him, he groaned and rolled off.

Fear shot through her. Had he changed his mind? "What? What is it?" she asked, her voice tinged with panic.

He rubbed a hand over his face. "I had no idea this would happen tonight. I mean, I guess I decided it might at Henry's but..."

"But what?"

"I don't have any protection." Staring up at the ceiling, he blew out a heavy breath. "We can't risk a pregnancy."

*Because he's leaving town.*

Her heart ached at the intrusion of reality. The very good chance that Jack would never allow himself this close to her again brought tears to her eyes. And frankly, the thought of having Jack's child didn't freak her out, despite the fact that she'd never given being a mother a moment's consideration. All she'd ever wanted to be was a vet. But to have a part of Jack forever in her life...

He'd never allow it. She knew as sure as she knew her name that he would get up and walk away before he took the risk. And that would be the end of it.

A flash of memory sent a bolt of relief and excitement through her.

"Oh! Wait. I just might..." She rolled to the other side of the bed and flipped up the white table topper covering the beat-up nightstand she'd used during college. She pulled out the lone, slender drawer and felt beneath the forgotten vet journals and a shallow box of tissue.

"Aha!" she extorted when her hand connected with a length of cool plastic. She pulled the long string of forgotten condoms from the drawer and held them up triumphantly.

He arched a brow at her.

"From college." She checked the expiration date. "They're still good."

His other brow went up.

She heaved an exasperated breath. "Remember the guy I told you about who—"

"Needs to have his face pounded in? Yeah, I remember." He rolled back toward her and pulled her tight against him. Leaning down, he looked directly into her eyes. "I'm glad he never had the chance to use those with you."

She felt compelled to explain, "There were originally more of them, Jack."

He curled his lip in a look of jealousy that sent her spirits soaring. "A guy like that could never deserve a woman like you, Melinda." He dropped a gentle, heart-rendingly tender kiss on her lips.

Her heart swelled with love for him and crowded the air from her lungs.

Raising his head, he reached for the packets. "Well, I'm glad I don't have to suffer through the, er, ribbing I'd have taken at The Mercantile for buying a case or two of these at a dead run."

She pulled back her chin. "You were going to go buy some? Tonight?"

"Damn straight. In case you haven't noticed," he rubbed his erection against her hip. "I want this, Melinda. I want you. Right here, right now. You game?"

Her throat tightened so much with love for him that she couldn't speak, so she nodded and slipped her arms around his smooth, strong shoulders.

Jack kissed her once, hinting at what he might do to her with his tongue, before pulling away long enough to put one of the condoms on. Then he was back, covering her with his body, his hands, his mouth. This time he blazed a new trail down her belly, not stopping until he was kissing and licking her exactly where she wanted him the most. The reality of what his tongue could do to her was incredible in ways beyond her imaginings.

But it wasn't enough. She wanted him to feel the same spiraling need. She tugged at his hair until he was kissing his way back up to mouth. The urgency returned to his touch, and it was only a matter of moments before he was there, inside of her, filling her so completely that she realized just how empty she'd been before.

He groaned and held himself still. "You feel so good. Man, I—" he stopped and groaned again when she tilted her pelvis up. She couldn't bear not moving against him. He reached down and slipped his hands beneath her hips, anchoring her to him. And when she wrapped herself completely around him with both arms and legs, as he'd wrapped himself around her heart, he gave into the intensity of their connection and made love to her like a man starved for release, like the man she knew he'd been for too long.

His power and need took her to a place she'd never been before, shamed her for thinking she'd ever felt anything near true ecstasy.

Or true love.

When she couldn't hold off any longer and wave after wave of exquisite release coursed through every cell in her body, intensified by Jack's own shuddering climax—punctuated by an ego boosting shout—she knew in the pit of her soul that Jack Hartman, wounded or not, was the only man she'd ever want again.

JACK IDLY RUBBED the pad of his thumb over the silky curl twined around his index finger as Melinda slept soundly in his arms. After they'd made love a second time, they'd finally crawled beneath the covers and Melinda had settled her head on his shoulder and promptly fell asleep.

Too much had changed today for him, though. Despite feeling completely content for the first time in five long years, he couldn't sleep. He'd known he'd find a haven of sorts in Melinda's arms, but he was stunned by the intensity of the need and passion she stirred in him. Emotions he didn't particularly want to examine too closely.

He'd been set on a certain path for so long that this sudden fork, this different choice, was hard to wrap his mind around. Could he actually stay in Jester? Stay with Melinda? The possibility was too extreme, too unexpected to handle right now. Especially with her dark blond hair looking like solid honey wrapped around his finger and her soft breasts pressed against his side as if she'd never been apart from him.

He couldn't just up and change his plans overnight.

But he also couldn't deny what he'd found so unexpectedly in Melinda's arms. Perhaps what everyone had been explaining away as him not being finished mourning Caroline was simply loneliness. Now he knew why he'd felt such a kinship with that stray dog. They'd both been left separate, alone, by circumstances beyond their control.

If Melinda could chase that feeling away, even just temporarily, didn't he owe it to himself to find out how long the feeling might last?

She murmured something in her sleep that sounded remarkably like *pigs,* then shifted a leg up over his, wrapping herself around him yet again. A heat spawned in his chest and spread outward, warming him and filling up places that had been cold for a very long time. Whether being with Melinda was right or not, having her in his arms, in his life, was certainly worth the effort.

## Chapter Eleven

Jack woke up the next morning and discovered he was alone in Melinda's bed, but for the first time in years he didn't feel an emptiness inside that was echoed by the unused pillow beside him.

He didn't feel lonely.

He stretched, his back stiff from sleeping on her too-soft mattress. The rest of him felt pretty damn good, though. Good enough, in fact, that he would have preferred to have Melinda within reach.

The flat, gray light of yet another snowy day barely eked through the crack between the pink curtains covering the window in Melinda's bedroom, so he figured it was early enough to convince her to come back to bed. Hopefully she'd only left to go to the bathroom. Naked. Maybe she'd even climbed into the shower.

An image of her gorgeous body all wet and sudsy had him sitting up and trying to throw the covers off, intending to hop out of bed to join her. But the covers wouldn't budge.

He realized he wasn't alone, after all.

One-Eyed Jack was lying on top of the comforter, his front paws curled under him, looking very much like a gray-and-black striped doorstop, staring at Jack with a single, unblinking yellow eye. There was something very accusatory in the way the cat stared at him.

"What? Did I wake you up?"

The cat didn't blink.

"Or maybe you think I'm horning in on your territory? That there's only room for one Jack in Melinda's life?" He leaned forward to bring his face closer to the battle-scarred feline, who didn't so much as twitch a whisker. "Well, I've got news for you, ol' One-Eye, you've got yourself some serious competition. That noise you heard last night was your mistress turning this old tomcat inside out. *Twice.* And I want her to do it again."

One-Eye finally blinked his one eye, and Jack automatically reached out and scratched the old guy's fat cheek. One-Eye leaned into Jack's hand and rumbled an irregular, broken sounding purr. "Yeah, I know. She's got heart enough for both of us, doesn't she."

There was a noise in the kitchen that sounded like a skillet being set on the stove, and Jack grumbled because his fantasy of showering with Melinda wasn't going to come true just yet. He pulled himself to the other side of the bed and got out, leaving One-Eye undisturbed. After yanking on his jeans, not bothering to button them up all the way because he didn't plan to wear them long, he headed for the kitchen.

He rounded the wall separating the living room
from the kitchen and stopped dead, heat flashing
through him. Melinda stood at the counter, wearing
nothing but his tan shirt with its tail brushing the
backs of her toned, bare thighs and her crazy fuzzy
gray socks on her feet. Her incredible hair hung in a
wild mess of curls down her back and her slender
calves flexed as she danced from one foot to the other
to the tune she was softly humming as she stirred
something in a bowl. He wasn't sure, but he thought
it might have been one of the songs they'd danced to
the other night at the saloon.

Then she surprised him by singing low in her throat
just like a rock singer, "Do me, do me, do me,"
gyrating her hips in time. Okay, so it wasn't one of
the songs they'd slow danced to.

As much as he would have liked to stand there and
watch her all morning, he couldn't contain the burst
of laughter her antics inspired.

She jumped. The spoon she'd been stirring with
clanked against the side of the glass bowl, and she
turned toward him with her mouth and eyes wide in
a mortified expression.

She really was a kick in the pants. He crossed his
arms over his bare chest all casual-like and propped
his shoulder against the end of the wall. "If I'd
known breakfast came with a floor show, I wouldn't
have slept so long."

She flushed prettily—and damn, she *was* pretty—
but made a good effort of appearing dignified by
throwing her chest out and raising her chin, which

actually only served to draw his attention to her ample breasts, their hardened tips clearly visible beneath the cotton shirt. The fact that it was *his* cotton shirt made him incredibly hot.

"I just happened to feel like singing this morning."

Testosterone producing pride surged through him for putting her in such a mood. He took a leisurely visual stroll from the top of her bed-messed hair down to her toasty looking footwear. "How about we postpone breakfast and let *me* entertain *you* for a while? In bed. Where we belong."

Her lips parted and her eyes took on a wistful, dreamy look like he'd offered up her favorite dessert. He made a mental note to find out what that was so he could feed it to her. In bed.

He uncrossed his arms, pushed off the wall and sauntered toward her, the hungry look in her eyes as she checked out his bare chest and open waistband making him harder yet. "It'd be interesting to discover what else you might feel like doing this morning."

She finally met his gaze, her eyes heavy-lidded and her mouth wearing a smile that most definitely counted as foreplay. "I just assumed you'd need some protein to keep up your strength. I can be pretty *demanding,* you know."

Jack slipped his arms around her waist and crowded her backward until he had her trapped between the counter and his rock hard front. She splayed her hands over his pecs, her warm touch raising delicious goose bumps across his bare skin. He dipped his head and nuzzled the silky area beneath her ear. "Man, you smell good."

"That's the pancake mix. I added a little vanilla to it."

"Oh. Well, in that case…" He reached behind her for the bowl of batter and dipped a finger in it. He brought his goopy finger up between them, but instead of tasting it as she clearly thought he was going to do judging by her slightly curled lip, he smeared the batter from the base of her throat as far down as the opening of the shirt would allow.

"Jack!" she protested, but when he dropped his head to lick off the batter, she giggled.

He grunted. "Doesn't taste nearly as good as it smells. Ah, hell. I guess I'm just going to have to haul you into the shower to clean it off." He tugged at her waist to encourage her to move away from the counter so he could lead her into the bathroom, but she gripped the edge of the counter and firmly anchored herself.

"Why is it I can't seem to feed you?"

"Because you're way more tempting." Because she wasn't inclined to leave the kitchen, he slipped his hands down to the silky smoothness of her thighs, teasing his fingertips along her skin and pushing the shirt up out of his way as he went. The question of whether or not she'd put underwear on suddenly became an erotic *must know*.

He searched the sable depths of her eyes, and while she might not know what he was thinking, the glint in her gaze made him hopeful that she was having erotic thoughts of her own. To think of all those times he'd glanced up from his paperwork and connected with her gaze without once having a sexual thought...

That sure as hell would never happen again.

When he reached the coolness of her bare bottom he grinned in triumph. Hell's bells, she made him hot.

He grabbed hold of her waist and hoisted her up onto the counter, her backside knocking the bowl out of the way with a clatter.

Her eyes widened momentarily, then she raised a saucy brow. "What about the shower?"

"Man, you're impatient." He nudged his way between her legs, loving the way he could feel her moist heat where he hadn't completely fastened his jeans. Thinking all sorts of wicked thoughts, namely how much he wanted to *do her* right here with her sitting on the counter, he reached for the top most button on her shirt and slipped it from its hole. "Got syrup?"

She made a half shocked, half delighted noise that had him grinning from ear to ear.

The phone rang, and she froze like she'd been caught doing something wrong.

"It's okay. We're engaged, remember?" he joked, then instantly wished he hadn't. He'd never imagined they would end up like this when he'd asked her to help him out. But try as he may, he couldn't make himself regret his choices.

Did she? Before he could search her face for an answer, she slipped off the counter and tried to step away from him, but the tail of the shirt caught on one of his jeans' unfastened button.

"Oh, jeez." Her laughter was nervous, maybe self-conscious. A far cry from the boasting temptress of a moment ago. He resented the intrusion from the outside world for more than one reason. He wanted to see more of this side of Melinda, and not just because it made him hot. She'd seemed as if she was really having fun, and she deserved a little fun in her life. They both did.

As she unhooked his shirt, he took the opportunity to duck down and catch her lips in what he hoped would be a reassuring kiss. She gave him a soft smile when he raised his head, then stepped away to answer the phone.

"Well, hello Mr. Anderson."

Jack dropped his chin. Roy Anderson had a very expensive horse that was very ready to foal. Because Roy had overseen more than his share of mares giving birth, his calling one of the town's vets was a bad sign. And the fact that he was one of the good old boys who didn't think a female vet could ever be worth her salt, his calling Melinda was an extremely bad sign.

She listened for a moment, her lips thinning, then turned to look at Jack. "Ah, well, why exactly do you need Dr. Hartman? Maybe I can help." Her blond brows came together sharply. "Mmm. Sure." Her delicate nostrils flared and she suddenly resembled a pissed bull. Damn those stubborn old men. "You know Mr. Anderson, here he is now. Why don't I just let you talk to him." She shoved the phone at Jack.

He blew out a breath and took the phone from her. "Morning, Roy."

"Jack, it's Miss May. She's been trying to foal for damn near thirty hours. That's way too long for her, and she's not looking good. I need you out here, Jack. I can't afford to lose this mare."

Miss May was the last direct descendent of Jester, the stallion, and thus was worth more than just money to the folks around here. "Understood, Roy. I'll get there as fast as I can." Jack fastened his gaze on Melinda, who'd crossed her arms over her chest and was trying to look uninterested. "And I'll bring Dr. Woods along for good measure."

Melinda glanced at him, but he couldn't tell if he was helping or hurting.

Roy sighed heavily over the phone. "If you need to. But I'm counting on you to deliver this foal, Jack."

"We'll see to it." Jack handed the phone back to Melinda and she hung it up none too gently.

It looked like playtime was over.

MELINDA TOOK the stethoscope from her ears. "The foal's not only wedged sideways, Jack, but its heart-beat is really slow and weak. It's definitely in distress. I think it might be tangled in its cord." She kept her voice low to keep it from carrying to wiry, sixty-something Roy Anderson hovering nervously in the stall door.

His sparse gray hair that must have at one time been coal-black was mussed as if he'd spent the past

thirty hours running his hands through it in worry and
frustration. His mare, Miss May, was extremely valu-
able, both financially and emotionally. Like many of
the ranchers around Jester, a good portion of his in-
come came from breeding and selling the offspring
of a few animals with excellent bloodlines. Miss
May's were some of the best, traced all the way back
to the original Jester, himself.

Jack removed his hand from within the exhausted
mare and sat back on his heals. His gaze troubled and
his jaw rigid, he wiped the sweat from his brow with
the rolled-up sleeve of his sweat darkened tan shirt.
"Damn it." He laid a rubber-gloved hand on the
mare's quivering flank. "She's been at it such a long
time, she's used up everything she had. Even with
our help, I'm not sure she can push her baby out in
time."

Melinda grimaced, hating when things went this
bad. "Emergency C?"

He glanced quickly at Mr. Anderson, then met her
gaze, his eyes shadowed with a look she'd never seen
before. "By the time we prep'ed, we'd be too late for
the foal, if it's been deprived of oxygen, but we need
to save the mare." He cursed violently beneath his
breath, then yanked the gloves from his hands and
stood. "I'll tell Roy."

Melinda ran her hands over the bulging stomach of
the mare, her hide wet and quivering from pain and
exhaustion. "Oh, Miss May. I'm so sorry." The foal
was so close, but Jack was right; it had been too long.

Miss May's chestnut coat was darkened with sweat,

the flesh around her eyes and muzzle sunken. And instead of pacing around the stall, lying down only to get back up again, as would have been natural, the mare had been flat out on her side since their arrival, her pregnant belly huge.

Melinda's gaze caught on her own slender hand and a thought occurred to her. All might not be lost. She opened her mouth and turned to tell the men as much, but the words died in her throat. Jack was consoling Mr. Anderson with a hand on his shoulder. What if she was wrong? Was it fair to get their hopes up?

Having spent a lifetime letting her actions speak for her, she closed her mouth and yanked a pair of long rubber gloves from the stash she always kept in her work coat pocket. As she peeled off her coat and pulled the gloves on, she moved past Miss May's quaking hind legs and positioned herself at the mare's rump. With a reassuring hand holding Miss May's top rear leg, in case she reflexively kicked, Melinda went fishing for a baby horse.

Her small hand and slender wrist and elbow were definitely assets in this instance, allowing her to reach far enough up to feel the cord and loosen it so that she could gently turn the foal. Melinda hoped her physical strength would prove an equal measure of her stubbornness, and strained until sweat gathered between her breasts and plastered the curls that had escaped her ponytail to her neck and forehead.

Her intrusion seemed to rouse the mare from her stupor, and with the next contraction, Miss May bore down, rumbling like distant thunder deep in her barrel chest with the effort. Melinda worked her fingers around until she felt sure she had a hold of the foal's slender front fetlocks just above the little hooves.

Before Melinda could position herself to pull, the mare's huge stomach muscles tightened as she fought to expel the foal, and it felt as if every bone in Melinda's hand and wrist was being crushed. She must have cried out, because Jack and Mr. Anderson rushed back into the stall.

Jack dropped to his knee next to her. "Melinda—"

"I have it, Jack! I've got it turned. I just need one more—" Another incredibly intense contraction gripped the mare and Melinda pulled downward at the same time. Her wrist, then two white membrane-encased hooves emerged, followed by two spindly legs.

The mare raised her head and looked back at Melinda and Jack, her huge brown eye moist and soft. Mr. Anderson knelt down and supported her head, chanting encouragements. Jack took hold of the delicate legs also to help, and the foal was born with a steaming wet rush right in Melinda's lap.

The baby horse lay limp, and Melinda snatched up one of the clean towels they'd readied earlier and hurried to clear its nostrils, mouth and throat while Jack unwound the umbilical cord from around the foal's narrow withers so it could break off naturally. But the baby still hadn't moved, hadn't taken its first breath. Melinda fought to contain a sob. To come so close—

Jack vigorously rubbed its chest to stimulate it,

then the foal lurched, stiffening all four spindly legs before it pulled in a gurgling breath. Soon it was breathing steadily and struggling to stand.

As if responding to her baby's movement, Miss May tucked her legs beneath her and rolled onto her belly to better see what was going on behind her. She was too exhausted to stand, so Jack rolled her over a little again and pushed the foal toward its mother's teat to stimulate the recovery process for them both.

Mr. Anderson whooped, patting his mare's slick neck.

Jack laughed in triumph. "You did it, Melinda! You did it. But how?"

Joy and relief swamped her and her eyes filled with tears. She pulled the gloves off with a snap and held up a hand. "Small hands. I knew if I could just get up in there far enough, I'd be able to turn the foal."

"Why in the hell didn't you say so earlier?"

"I...well, I wasn't sure...."

"Sure or not, you should have said something. It was a sight better than giving up. Like I did." He turned to Mr. Anderson. "Did you happen to notice who just saved your mare and her foal?"

Roy Anderson met her gaze, an expression she'd never seen in his eyes before—respect. "That I did, Jack. And I'm in her debt. You can see to my animals any time, Dr. Woods."

A flush of heat spread from Melinda's chest up her neck and into her cheeks. It took her a moment to identify the emotion providing the fuel to the incredible warmth.

Satisfaction.

She felt incredibly satisfied because she'd just *earned* the respect for her work as a veterinarian that she'd craved so desperately. Tears blurred her vision. She busied herself wiping the foal, a filly that favored her gorgeous dam down to the same white sock on her hind right leg, so the men wouldn't see her womanly show of emotion.

What a weekend she was having. First her fantasy about making love with Jack comes true in a mind-blowing way, then she'd been given the best compliment possible from Mr. Anderson. And because he was good friends with Bud Webster and many of the other residents of Jester, his praise might go a long way toward changing some opinions about female vets.

Things were sure going her way. Maybe she should buy a lottery ticket of her own.

There was a very real chance that before long, her quest for respect here in Jester would be realized.

Jack's part of their deal would be met.

And he'd be free to leave.

A pall settled over her mood. If she had done nothing, if she hadn't acted to save the mare and her foal, Jack might have had to stay in town longer. She wouldn't have to count on what she was afraid was a tenuous attraction to her to keep him in town, he'd still be held by his honor. They'd made a deal, after all. But no matter how much she wanted Jack in her life, she could never risk an animal's life to keep him there.

She would just have to risk using what she had to offer him as a woman to keep him in Jester. If only she hadn't spent her entire life ignoring what she had to offer, she might feel more confident about convincing him that she was worth staying for.

What a fool she'd been thinking that she'd be able to handle him leaving.

## Chapter Twelve

"I don't care if you're sure or not, I want you to speak up." Jack shifted his gaze from the icy road as he drove them home from the Anderson ranch and looked her square in the eye. His green eyes held a flinty hardness she'd never seen directed at her before.

Coupled with the day's growth of whiskers he hadn't been able to shave off this morning, he had an incredibly masculine and intense beauty about him that made her mouth go dry.

"I expect you to, Melinda. As my partner in this practice, I expect you to offer any knowledge, experience or skill you have that I don't. Okay?"

Pride infused her with heat and the flush that had been heating her chest since Jack had insisted broaching the subject the moment they'd headed home migrated to her cheeks. "Okay."

Even though he returned his attention to the road, she shifted in the passenger seat, her habitual urge to clam up warring with the connection she now felt with Jack forged by their intimacy. Since today had already been a day chock-full of risks, what was one more? It would only be one more piece of her heart that he'd take with him, but if she didn't start letting him in, she'd lose him for sure.

She lowered her voice self-consciously. "But it's hard for me, Jack."

"Why?" he shot right back at her without so much as a pause. Apparently he had no intention of making it easy for her.

She pulled in a deep breath. "My mom doesn't want to talk about much besides the weather and the farm, and my dad never really wanted to hear what I had to say. Over time, it became easier to let him see the end result of my ideas rather than attempting to get his attention long enough to express them. Assuming he noticed the end results, that is."

He looked at her, the glint in his eyes softening. "Which wasn't often?"

She forced a laugh in an attempt to hide how much she still cared about her father's lack of interest in her and how much Jack's understanding meant to her. "No. Not often."

"Well, Melinda," he drawled, shifting his attention back to the road. "You can't so much as breathe without me noticing, so do me a favor and speak up when you have an idea. Especially a lifesaving idea." He looked back at her. "Understand?"

Her embarrassment turned to soul-healing pleasure. For the first time she mattered to someone without much of a fight. "Understood, Jack."

A corner of his mouth turned up wickedly as he quickly looked ahead, then back at her. "Good, because I'd hate to think there was a spot on you that you really liked to have kissed but I missed it and you never 'fessed up.''

Her toes curling in her work boots, Melinda grinned in return. ''Actually, now that you mention it...'' she trailed off and giggled. Tingling anticipation built in the pit of her stomach.

Jack smiled broadly. ''What! Where? Tell me now, woman, or I'll stop this truck right here in the middle of the road and go looking for it.'' He reached a big hand toward her and made a playful grab for the hem of the dry, spare sweatshirt and sweatpants she'd changed into in Mr. Anderson's tack room after they'd finished up with Miss May and her new foal. Dirt and manure were one thing to track into a truck, but there were some things even vets preferred not to wear home, so they each kept an easily packed change of clothes in their gear.

She squealed and lurched away from him, squashing herself against the passenger door. ''I don't think Luke would appreciate us being the source of an actual traffic jam on the road into town. And while Nathan and Conner wouldn't be all that surprised if we showed up at the medical clinic with frostbite, they *would* wonder how we got it on, shall we say, *delicate* places?''

''Delicate? There's nothing delicate on me, little lady. I would have thought you'd have noticed that last night.''

Loving their play, she straightened up in her seat and reached a hand to his muscular thigh. ''Oh, I noticed all sorts of things last night, Jack. But it was so dark, and you kept making these whimpering sorts of sounds...."

He took a hand from the wheel and grabbed hers, sliding it higher on his taut thigh until her hand rested on a different sort of hardness. "We need to get your hearing checked, then, because that was no whimper, darlin', that was a *roar*."

Her temperature rising in response to his obvious interest, she leaned closer to him, able to pick out the strangely enticing scent of his sweat and the remnants of his spicy aftershave over the antiseptic soap smell. "Really? Hmm. You know, the acoustics aren't that good in my bedroom, with all that *girly* stuff in there, but I imagine the shower would be better for determining—"

Jack made a very distinct, definite growling noise and released her hand so he could reach up and pull her toward him for a quick but incredibly intense kiss that turned the tingling anticipation in her stomach into a burning need and steamed the windows.

His whiskers were rough against her chin, adding an unnecessary reminder that he'd been in her bed this morning instead of at home where he could shave. She reflexively curled her fingers around his arousal as much as she could through his jeans, responding to his hard heat with a damp warmth of her own.

He released her just as quickly and focused again on driving. "You read my mind, darlin'."

She snuggled against him as best she could while

still buckled in for the remainder of the ride back to her place, which thankfully wasn't far. His gentlemanly manners losing out in the face of her sexual needs, she didn't wait for him to open the door for her. Instead, she grabbed her bag from between her feet, hopped out of his truck the moment it stopped in her driveway and made a beeline for the side door of her house. Jack was fast on her heels.

No matter how anxious they were to get in the shower together, they were both sensible enough to take their soiled clothes from the plastic bags they'd brought them home in and put them in the washer. Jack earned still more points by checking on Melinda's animals while she added soap to the washer and got it going.

She tried to make it to the bathroom first to freshen up, but Jack came up behind her in the hall and engulfed her.

His kisses were everywhere. On her neck, her ear, beneath her jaw. They were so distracting in their incongruent lusty sweetness that she didn't realize he was also untying the string holding her baggy gray sweatpants up until they dropped around her ankles as she turned into the bathroom.

She laughed, only to have the sound muffled when he pulled the matching sweatshirt up over her head and flung it into the sink. Then he was in front of her and his lips found hers, and his play gave way to a seriousness reflected in the almost reverent way he slipped his big, blunt fingers beneath her white bra straps and pushed them off her shoulders.

With a deft flick he unfastened the clasp and she let the bra drop to the cool white linoleum. His mouth continued to tantalize hers as his hands stripped her white cotton underwear from her with the same ease, though he spent more time gliding his callused fingertips over the sensitive skin of her bottom, raising goose bumps in his wake.

He nibbled his way out of the kiss and said, "You're cold. I better get you under some warm water." He stepped away from her and reached past the white shower curtain with blue paw prints to turn the shower on. Melinda did shiver then, chilled without his heat and feeling self-conscious with him still fully clothed.

Jack took care of that discrepancy in short order, whipping his clothes off as only a man can. His eyes hot on her, he tested the water, then took her hand and guided her into the tub like she was royalty. Which royally turned her on.

The second he joined her, turning so the spray of water hit them both, she plastered herself to his broad chest, grabbed the back of his neck and pulled him down for the most telling kiss she could give him. She boldly explored his tongue with hers, stroking and thrusting like she wanted him to do to her. Jack rumbled something deep in his throat, the sound unmistakably appreciative, and gathered her into his arms so that they touched everywhere. They fit perfectly together. It felt so right. So very, very real.

Tears pricked the backs of Melinda's eyes. He had

to care for her, he had to. She couldn't believe he could hold her, kiss her this way if he didn't.

He backed her against the cool tile, taking command of the kiss. When he hitched her leg around his hip, Melinda stopped thinking.

His hands on her bottom, he lifted her completely so she could wrap both legs around his hips. He risked fate by making love to her hard, fast and deep, pulling out at the last second after riding her climax to the end. Only then did it dawn on her that he hadn't put a condom on.

She met his turbulent gaze in the muted light within the shower and knew that he'd nearly forgotten about it, also.

Breathing hard, he settled his wet forehead against hers. "Damn. I can't believe what I almost just did. You get me so hot. I'm sorry."

"It wasn't just you, Jack. I'm a big girl. But I was caught up in the moment, too."

He dipped his head and licked the water streaming down her neck. "Some moment, eh?"

Feeling languid, she tilted her head back to give him better access. "I'll say."

"Want to do it again?"

"I knew there was a reason why I like you so much, Jack."

This time he was torturously leisurely in his lovemaking, taking extreme care not to miss a single spot on her body with the bar of soap he glided over her. She tried to do her part by washing him, but when he wouldn't give up the bar of soap, she was forced to settle for rubbing her soapy parts against his parts. By the time the water grew undeniably cold, they were both very clean, very pruney and very turned on again.

Jack added fuel to the fire by taking his time drying her off, alternately rubbing and patting his way from the top of her head to the tips of her toes with one of her oversized, white bath towels. He even went as far as licking certain sensitive spots so he'd have an excuse to dry them again. While she felt more cared for than she had her entire life, she was also more aroused than she'd ever been before.

She snatched another towel from the bar near the tub and dropped to her knees, intent on doing a little drying of her own.

Jack made a very grateful sound in the back of his throat and let her have her way with him for all of two minutes, then he snatched her up and carried her to bed. They made love again, but this time they did it slow, safe, and soulfully.

And as Melinda held his shuddering body tight against her, she vowed to make him realize just how right they were together, how much he belonged here with her in Jester.

THE NEXT MORNING Melinda sat across from Jack in a booth at The Brimming Cup and she lost herself in his gaze the same way she used to fall into a beckoning pile of freshly cut sweet alfalfa. She knew the landing would be just as soft and the carefree abandon just as rewarding. At least, for the moment.

The moment was broken, however, when the mayor's loud, self-grandiose voice calling for everyone's attention accompanied his arrival in the diner with Paula and her ever-present clipboard during working hours mincing in his wake. "May I have everyone's attention, please!" Bobby looked more like a used-car salesman, or a refugee from the golf movie *Caddyshack,* than usual in a white sport coat and green, white-and-blue plaid pants.

Blocked from the customer she was about to serve a coffee refill to by the mayor's wide frame, Shelly planted a fisted hand on her hip and gave Bobby a baleful look. While conversation stopped, those with food in front of them continued to eat. Bobby would talk anyway.

"I have a very important announcement pertaining to our great town's annual Founders' Day celebration. I already delivered it formally to the media over at Town Hall, but since so many of you are here, I decided it wouldn't hurt to repeat myself."

Someone in the back, Dean, maybe, muttered loudly, "It might not hurt you, but it's killin' us."

Everyone except Bobby and Paula chuckled.

Bobby glanced at Paula, who gave him an encouraging nod. He pulled in a chest expanding breath. "After a tremendous amount of deliberation, I have determined that for the good of our town's image, which I have worked diligently to elevate since the lottery brought us worldwide attention, we will not be utilizing the pavilion this year."

That got people's attention.

Dean and Finn, looking incomplete without Henry in the back booth with them, talked simultaneously.

Dean said, "What do mean, 'not utilizing the pavilion'?"

Finn exclaimed, "Not use the pavilion?"

Shelly pointed in the general direction of the park with the coffeepot. "Where will the band play? They always play in the pavilion." Shelly was big on tradition, so much so that when her parents passed away, she'd stepped right into their life and took over the diner. Until Dr. Connor O'Rourke made her start living for herself again.

Irene, who'd been in the corner enticing baby Max over the edge of his playpen to crawl, wagged a finger at the mayor. "Bobby Larson—"

Paula cleared her throat and interjected, "*Robert* Larson."

Irene either didn't hear her or chose to ignore her. "That pavilion has been a part of the Founders' Day celebration since before you were born. Your father would have never dreamed of such a thing as not using the pavilion when he was mayor." Though Bobby was in his late-forties, Irene sounded as if she were scolding a child.

Despite a distinct flush creeping up his neck, Bobby waved them down with a patronizing air. "Now I know this is a deviation from tradition, but Jester is a new town, now, and we need to put a new face on our image, need to put our best foot forward. And that old pavilion ain't it. So I've decided we'll set up a bandstand of sorts in the middle of the park, so people can gather all around, providing better access for the news crews.''

Everyone started talking at once while Jack groaned and rolled his eyes. ''Great. Leave it to Bobby to turn everything into a circus.''

Dread gripped Melinda tight around the middle. She didn't want anything to make her job of convincing Jack to stay any harder than it already was. More media attention would not be a good thing. ''We don't have to go, you know.''

He blew out a breath, then rested his crossed arms on top of the table and leaned toward her, narrowing the distance between them. ''No. You can't miss your first Founders' Day celebration. Besides, folk come in from all around. It'll be a great opportunity for people to get to know you better, to help further entrench you in town. The sooner everyone starts thinking of you as a part of Jester, the sooner they'll accept you as their vet.''

Melinda slipped down into her seat. She hated that every time Jack talked about getting her accepted by the town she feared he was taking one step closer to making good on his plan to leave.

She didn't have much time to waste convincing him to stay.

If only she knew how.

Bobby raised his hands to reclaim everyone's attention. ''There's more, people.''

Dean called, ''Careful, Bobby. Don't want to wear yourself out.''

That sent snickers through the diner again. It wasn't

that Bobby Larson wasn't liked, he just wasn't *well* liked. He worked so hard at being who he was, or rather who he thought he should be—a greater man than his father had been—that he'd darn near turned himself into a caricature. Melinda felt sorry for him, knowing full well how hard it was to try to influence people's opinions.

Bobby cleared his throat and ignored Dean by using the heel of his hand to smooth back where his light brown hair had grayed at the temple. "I will be putting through legislation to expand the town of Jester, and will be drawing up plans to add a large hotel on the land that is now occupied by the community park. Which is why I want to assure that this Founders' Day celebration will be the best one yet, because it will be the last one held in the park. The Town Hall lawn should serve nicely in the future."

The diner fell eerily silent for the space of a moment or two, then erupted in noise as everyone talked at once again.

With her mouth hanging open at Bobby's audacity, Melinda turned to look at Jack. He was frowning as he took a sip of coffee. Apparently changing the town itself wasn't what Jack wanted. But would it help him stay? Would the memories be easier to bear if the town were different?

Melinda wished she knew if he still felt as haunted as he had before.

She was too afraid of the answer to ask.

## Chapter Thirteen

Melinda couldn't believe how abuzz Jester was over Mayor Bobby Larson's announcement during the week approaching Founders' Day. From what she could tell, the general consensus seemed to be that most were afraid Bobby was bringing about the end to their quiet, quaint town. That Jester wouldn't be Jester without its community park and "antique" pavilion. And no one disputed that a large hotel would change things for sure.

Life had certainly changed since the lottery win, but those changes had been for the better in most instances. There was hope where there used to be despair, contentment where there used to be stress and worry. The infusion of cash—a goodly portion of it coming from the media and curious out-of-towners— had returned a vitality to the town that had definitely been absent when Melinda had first arrived. She wanted to be a part of this town more than ever.

But she wanted Jack here with her, too.

He'd weathered Henry's funeral and burial in the Faulkner plot behind the church better than she had thought he would. Only his grip on her hand revealed his struggle dealing with the heartbreak of the moment and the memories the funeral stirred for him.

Melinda had been further surprised to discover Jack's late wife hadn't been buried in the Peterson plot, though they had held a memorial for her at the little church. When Jack had noticed Melinda looking at the grave markers there, wanting to say a prayer over the woman who'd been so important to him, he'd told her that Caroline's parents had wanted to bury her near them in Idaho. He'd been too overwhelmed with his grief to think to object.

Melinda had simply assumed that Caroline had been buried here, and that was one of the reasons Jack wanted to leave. When she found out differently, her guilt over wanting to keep him in Jester diminished considerably.

She wanted to make their engagement real. As real as it had felt all week as they'd worked together, ate together and made love together, with Jack only occasionally going to his house—and possibly his memories of what he'd lost before.

She tried with all her might not to worry that he could in some way be comparing her to Caroline, and she might be falling short. That left her to worry that he might not be emotionally moving on with his life after all, that he couldn't as long as he stayed in Jester. Yet the more she saw him interact with the people in town, obviously caring about them, the less guilty she felt about wanting him to stay with her here.

The morning of the celebration dawned clear and beautiful, despite a dire forecast of a blizzard on the way, due to hit later in the day. Figuring they could head home early if the weather did indeed turn for the worse, Jack had suggested they walk from Melinda's house to the park.

Bundled up tight against the ten-degree weather, a heat wave by some standards considering the time of year, they walked hand and hand out Melinda's door and down Mega-Bucks Boulevard toward Main Street, looking very much like a happy couple.

For Melinda it was so, so true.

This was exactly what she'd always dreamed a relationship with Jack would be like—no, that wasn't true. The sheer joy he inspired in her was beyond anything she could have imagined.

She pointed at the scaffolding and supplies that were beginning to stack up next to the little, white, nondenominational church across the street as preparations for repairing its currently snow-covered slanted roof were made. The chimney, fascia boards and stained glass window had already reaped the benefits of the church's benefactor. "Shelly isn't wasting any time, is she?"

Jack looked at the church. "Nope. After everyone made it clear on her job board which project they wanted her to fund with a portion of her winnings, she got right to it."

"That's incredibly generous of her."

Jack shrugged. "That's Shelly. Though I have to say, pretty much every one of the winners has some plan or another that will benefit the town in some way.''

*That's because they intend to stay.*

The thought was a crushing weight on Melinda's chest, but she pushed it away, not wanting anything to ruin such a glorious day. Or her happiness. She'd waited too long to finally experience this sort of joy, and she was going to cling to it as long as she could. She needed to live in the moment, take in the beauty around her. There was a bright clarity to the snow-encased world that only happened when it was dang cold outside.

Jack's gaze remained on the opposite side of the street as they neared the corner where Main Street formed a T with Mega-Bucks Boulevard, and when they were directly across from the green statue of Caroline Peterson sticking like glue to a bucking Jester, he stopped, his expression unreadable.

Without looking at her he asked, ''Have I ever told you the true story behind how that horse was tamed?''

She raised her brows. Of course he hadn't. They never talked of anything that was remotely connected to his late wife. But all she said was, ''No, I don't think you have.''

He gestured at the statue. ''There wasn't a whole lot of bucking involved, that's for sure. The story, as it's told among the Peterson women, is that this particular Caroline was the only human Jester would let near him without a fight, mainly because she kept her pockets stuffed with sugar cubes, or clumps, or whatever they had back then. She simply won him over with patience and sweets.''

Melinda nodded at the pioneer Caroline's wisdom. Maybe that was where Melinda had gone wrong with Jack. She'd been plenty patient, but she'd never baked for him. She suppressed a grin at the thought of what making soup for him had garnered her.

"You know," he mused. "I should use some of my money to get that statue cleaned up. It certainly needs it.''

A wild flutter started in Melinda's chest. Jack wanted to spend some of his *moving money* on fixing up the very symbol of Jester, the statue of his late wife's ancestor and namesake? Granted, he had more than enough money, but his wanting to spend some to restore what had to be the biggest reminder of what he'd lost was stunning. Did he mean it as a final tribute to his late wife? Or was it because Jack was coming to terms with the past?

The flutter turned into a bucking bronco of her own as hope flooded her. She squeezed his hand. "That would be a very fine thing to do, Jack."

He looked at her, and she met his gaze. There were a lot of feelings muddying his green eyes—regret, pain, she thought—but there was also acceptance. Melinda could hardly breathe around the relief crowding her chest.

He gave a brief, firm nod. "Then it's settled." His deep baritone sounded scraped, but was still strong and sure.

Her smile came straight from her heart, but she

didn't care. If he happened to notice, to realize how deeply she loved him, then so be it. Because as they started walking again, turning the corner and heading down Main Street toward the park two blocks away and the crowd they could see already gathering, Melinda decided that today was the day. Come hell or blizzard, she was going to ask Jack to stay with her in Jester and make their engagement real.

She believed in the pit of her soul that Jack was finally healing, finally ready to begin his life again. His support and insistence she speak up gave her the courage to fight for what she wanted. To just flat-out say what it was.

She wanted Jack.

THE STRANGEST SORT of peace settled over Jack as he walked down Main Street hand in hand with Melinda. Then it hit him. He was *happy*. Completely happy for the first time in five years. The loneliness that had been mistaken as mourning by those around him was well and truly gone.

He waited for the guilt he'd dreaded for so long would come with feeling this way. But it didn't come. His chest simply continued to fill with warmth, and what could only be described as contentment. Damn, he felt good.

He automatically glanced at Melinda, who had a small, contented sort of smile of her own curling the corners of her lovely mouth. He looked away and focused again on their destination. While he was willing to own his happiness, he wasn't quite ready to admit to the possible reasons behind it. He still needed to take one step at a time.

When they reached the park they were immediately engulfed by a welcoming, family atmosphere that was Jester at its best. He couldn't tell if anyone noticed if his handshake was a little firmer, his smile more heartfelt. But while the Montana ground still lay firmly frozen, a thaw had begun inside of him, and he was nearly light-headed with relief. The loneliness that had gripped him for so long had nearly squeezed the life right out of him, and it felt so good to have that life back.

Luke came up to them, his blue eyes sharp and clear again beneath the shadow of his Stetson, unlike the last time Jack had seen him at Henry's funeral. "Hey, Jack. Caught the dog, yet?"

"No, I haven't. And I don't expect to this weekend." Jack surveyed the park, full of people and balloons and music and food. Lots and lots of food.

He breathed in deep the heavenly smells of carnival, Montana style. There were barbecue beef ribs cooking somewhere, and Jack's mouth started to water. "There's going to be enough spilled kettle corn, hot dogs and discarded ribs to make that dog think he's died and gone to doggie heaven. He'll be full for a month."

Luke grunted in agreement. "I just hope he waits until everyone has cleared out before he comes slinking in. I'd hate to have someone unrack the rifle in their truck and pop him, thinking he's a wolf."

Jack blew out a foggy breath. "Hopefully the noise

will keep him away. If he were hungry enough to risk the crowd, he would have gone after the bait in the trap by now.''

''Probably right.'' Luke turned his gaze on Melinda, the appreciation on his face raising Jack's hackles in a surprisingly intense way. He blinked at the realization he was jealous. Something else he hadn't felt in a very long time, whether he should or not.

Luke used the tip of a blunt finger to push his cowboy hat upward. ''Melinda, I heard ol' Jester's line lives on thanks to you. Roy Anderson is talking you up to anyone who'll listen for saving his mare and foal. Atta girl.''

Melinda's cheeks, already pink from the cold, colored more. Jack's chest swelled with pride. Not only was she the most gorgeous thing around with her long, dark blond curls dancing in the wind and her chestnut eyes sparking with pleasure, she was a hell of a fine vet. And she was finally getting the recognition she deserved.

He was glad for an entirely different reason than he would have been a couple of weeks ago. Before he wanted her happy so she would stay in Jester and take over his practice, now he wanted her happy because he cared about her. But he didn't want to think about how deeply right now. He simply wanted to enjoy this day. To just live. With Melinda's hand tucked securely within his.

Luke gestured at her head. ''I never realized how long your hair was. It looks real good down like that.''

Melinda smiled and dropped her gaze to the ground. "Thank you, Sheriff."

Jack planted his splayed hand in the middle of Luke's chest and applied a steady pressure. "Don't you have some community policing to do, or vendor licenses to check or something?"

Luke grinned at him and yielded to the pressure, a knowing twinkle in his blue eyes as he stepped backward. "Okay, okay. You two have fun."

Jack snaked an arm around Melinda and drew her tight against him. "No worries there."

Luke pointed a finger at them. "Hey. Keep the PDA to a minimum. This is a family event, after all." He changed his admonishment to a wave. "Here's hoping the weather holds. See ya," he said and sauntered away toward the low, temporary stage the mayor had ordered constructed in the center of the park's green space. Kids of various sizes were climbing onto it and readying their band instruments, not an easy thing on a subfreezing day.

Melinda cocked a brow at Jack. "PDA?"

He bent his head toward her until the steam their breath generated in the cold air mingled. "Public Display of Affection." Then he demonstrated by catching her lips with his for a hard, quick kiss before straightening away from her.

She smiled as brightly as the sun reflecting off the frozen pond. "Ah."

"Come on. Let's go get some hot cider and something to eat before the band finishes thawing their instruments." He tugged her toward where food booths had been set up on the basketball courts. But they couldn't go far without stopping to visit with someone.

Irene had her little twelve-year-old tan Welsh Corgi, Benny, with her, outfitted in a light blue, knitted doggie sweater that matched her scarf. After greeting Irene, Jack dropped down in a squat to check the old fella's joints.

"Hey, Benny. How you doing?"

The little dog nudged his long muzzle along Jack's jeans-encased thigh and wagged his bottom for all he was worth.

Jack looked up at Irene, squinting against the winter sun. "He moving okay?"

Irene pulled her scarf down from her chin. "He's a little stiff when he first gets up, but after he gets going, he seems to move fine. He never was much of a speed demon, you know."

Considering Benny was of a breed that had very short legs and stocky bodies, that was understandable, but they had been developed to help herd livestock. Still, Jack knew Benny had been more of a porch dog than a work dog, especially after the death of Irene's husband.

With a last pat to the dog, Jack stood, and Irene looked between him and Melinda with a merry twinkle in her blue eyes. "So, do we have a date, yet? Or any other specifics? I'm just dying to help out." She put a quick gloved hand to Melinda's arm. "You will let me help out, won't you? I have the best bean casserole I can make for the reception. Or maybe an engagement party?''

Melinda smiled sweetly at Irene. ''I promise we won't do a thing without your help, Irene.''

Jack nodded in agreement. He no longer felt a twinge of guilt over the truth of their engagement. He supposed the fact that they were at least physically involved made the lie less bitter. At least, that's how he chose to rationalize how he felt.

When they finally got their food, their choice was affected by what they could eat with their gloves on. They settled on hot cider and hot dogs that, by mutual agreement after a lot of eyebrow wiggling and snickers, they'd left the onions off of. Food in hand, they found an empty picnic table amongst those that had been hauled out from the pavilion and scattered around the park. They sat side-by-side and started right in on their food before the freezing air cooled it completely.

Melinda remarked, ''You know, Jack, I don't think it would be an exaggeration to say that you know just about everyone in this town.''

He shrugged at the obviousness of it. ''It's a town of pet owners. Nathan and Connor probably know everyone, too. Though far more...personally than I do.''

''And you like everyone.''

He did. But liking and belonging were two different things. Though the thought of leaving town didn't hold near the urgency it previously had. And he knew why. ''Jester's a town of good people, Melinda.''

She fell silent while they finished eating their hot dogs. They listened to the small, multigrade band from the school play and chatted with people who stopped by to wish them well.

Though the day only warmed up to the low teens, Melinda's color continued to run high, repeatedly drawing his attention to her beautiful face. He finally leaned over and whispered, "You've been glowing all day. Have you been thinking about being on top again?"

She blinked, then elbowed him. "Shh, Jack. Remember what Luke said about this being a family event."

"I can't help it. You're too gorgeous."

Her big brown eyes misted, and she launched herself at him, wrapping her arms around his neck and squeezing.

Contentment squeezed him from the inside, and he tried to lighten the moment for both their sakes by joking, "Oh, boy. PDA, PDA. You're going to get us busted."

Her heart near to exploding with the love she felt for Jack, Melinda gave him one more hard squeeze for being so dang wonderful, then pulled away. And after seeing the evidence of all the friendships he had here, she knew it was time. She had to find out if there was even the slimmest chance of them making a life together in Jester.

She stood. "Then we better go find us a not-so-public spot. Come on." She held out a hand, and he took it in his, his grip wonderfully warm and possessive.

"I *do* like the way you think, Dr. Woods." He stood. "Lead on."

Hoping it would indeed be a private spot, Melinda led Jack straight to the pavilion. The space beneath the old gazebo like roof seemed even colder without the picnic tables at least giving the concrete pad visual warmth, if nothing else. And thanks to the wind that was steadily picking up, it was like stepping into a cooler. The mayor had been adamant that no activities take place beneath the cover, feeling that it would blight Jester's new and improved image.

But Melinda couldn't think of a better place to plead her case than where she and Jack had shared their first kiss. The hot look in Jack's eyes made her believe he was thinking about that night also.

As soon as they'd taken a few steps on the concrete pad he pulled her into his arms. She was instantly enveloped in warmth. God, how she loved him.

He reached up and cupped her face, drawing her away from his chest so he could lean down and kiss her. She kissed him back, but when he sought to deepen the kiss, she stepped away. She didn't want passion to muddle what she wanted to say.

"What's wrong?"

"Nothing," she automatically replied, but she backed away. She gave him a smile that was shaky around the edges. This was going to be so hard for her, and she dearly prayed this was the right thing to do. But he had said he wanted her to speak up, right?

He closed the distance she'd put between them and reached for her hands. It wasn't until he pried them apart that she realized she'd been wringing them. "This doesn't look like nothing." He'd used his soothing voice. The one that gave her strength.

"Well, I guess there is something. Something I want to ask you, that is."

"What is it, sweetheart?"

His endearment was just the shot of courage she needed. He cared for her, she knew he did. Just as she knew he cared about this town, about the people in it. All she needed to do was get him to realize it. But she couldn't think clearly with him so near. She slipped her hands from his and paced to the center of the empty pavilion.

She finally turned and found him watching her with a wary look that turned his eyes a mossy green. Did he suspect what she was about to say? It didn't matter, because this was the perfect time, the perfect place. Jack seemed ready to hear what she had to say and her heart couldn't bear going one more day without saying it.

"Jack, I want to make our—" The pavilion groaned loudly and cut her off as a particularly strong gust of biting wind buffeted it before dying down. Melinda raised her brows and glanced up at the large, rough-hewn beams that met in the center like the spokes of a wheel and were held in place by metal brackets over her head. Everything looked fine, so she shrugged and shifted her attention back to Jack.

Before she could speak, the air was rent by the high pitched squeal of wood slipping against steel.

Jack jerked his gaze upward, and Melinda followed suit. The trusses holding the center of the roof together seemed to be shifting, like the wind was blowing them out of place. Which was odd, because the wind wasn't blowing at the moment—

Jack shouted something, and she dropped her gaze to him in time to see the look of horror evolving on his handsome face as he lunged toward her. But before his words could register, the world above her exploded in ear-splitting noise, the beams fell and she was driven to the ground by searing pain and darkness.

# Chapter Fourteen

Jack realized with horror that the roof of the pavilion was collapsing and he tried to warn Melinda, to get to her, but it happened too fast. His heart stalled in terror as he watched. In the blink of an eye and with a roar that didn't quit in his ears, the beams that had met in the center of the roof came down on top of Melinda, hitting her on the head along with a seemingly endless amount of snow. But because the outer supports remained upright, the entire structure didn't fall.

Boards and snow rained down on him, too, but he never took his eyes off Melinda. Whether the rest was going to come down or not, Jack immediately threw himself at the edge of the pile of snow and ancient timbers Melinda lay beneath, clawing at it with a strength born of desperation.

*Please, God. Not Melinda. Not Melinda, too.*

He was nearly to her when he realized he wasn't alone. There were other hands helping him dig through the snow that had been building up on the roof of the pavilion all winter. Snow that was supposed to be scraped off after every heavy snowfall but hadn't been that winter. People were yelling and shouting instructions, but all he could hear was his own labored breathing, his own repeated prayer.

*Please God. Not Melinda. Not Melinda, too.*

He finally reached one of the large central timbers, pausing for just one horrendous moment when he saw Melinda's long hair fanned out on the concrete floor beneath it. But when he reached to lift the beam, he saw it wasn't actually on top of her. Something had stopped the timber before it had crushed her. Fearing it might still drop the last foot and a half and land on top of her, he fell to his knees and wedged his shoulder beneath the huge, rough-hewn beam.

It registered that Luke was there beside him, flat on his belly as he tried to get to Melinda. "She's alive!" Luke shouted. "And there's only one board actually on her. Somebody help me pull her out this way!"

Jack started to move out from under the support beam, but the second he dropped his shoulder, the beam shifted with him.

Luke popped his head up. "No Jack! Stay there. Don't move."

Nathan and Connor came into Jack's field of vision and got down to help Luke.

The beam lightened infinitesimally, and Jack turned his head and saw Dev and Dean straddling the timber and pulling it upward between their legs as best they could. They would never be able to keep it from crushing Melinda if it did shift and fall, however, so Jack did as Luke had commanded and stayed put, his heart pounding with dread.

Nathan, who was the smallest in stature of the three, scrambled under the debris the farthest. "I can't tell how badly hurt she is, but—"

"Ow." The ultimate understatement was definitely female and had come from within the rubble near all that wonderful blond hair.

Relief collapsed Jack's lungs the same way the snow had collapsed the roof, and he could only draw in shallow breaths. *Thank you.*

Nathan said, "Tell me where it hurts, Melinda."

"Where the roof hit me." All that was missing from her tone was a prolonged *duh*. She sounded okay.

His relief took hold, and Jack pulled in gulps of damp, cold, wood-tinged air.

Nathan chuckled. "Okay. It looks like there's just one board directly on top of you, so when I push it up, Luke and Connor will pull you out." He yelled, "You got that, guys?"

"Got it," Luke answered.

Melinda's voice quavered, "Where's Jack?"

He shouted, "I'm right here, sweetheart!" Damn it. He should be the one under there with her. The inability to be the one at her side, soothing her, *saving her* resurrected all the feelings of helplessness he'd had the last time he'd been trapped in a waking nightmare.

When Caroline had died. When he hadn't been able to see her, let alone save her and their unborn child.

"He's busy holding up the house," Nathan answered.

She made a soft, scoffing sort of noise. "He does have an Atlas complex, you know." The thinness of her voice belied her brave joking.

Connor said to Luke, "I'll stabilize her neck, and you reach under my arms and get a hold of her armpits. If you can, just slide her along the ground. Keep her as flat as possible."

"Ready, guys?" Nathan called.

Wedging themselves next to Jack so they could be in a crouched position, Connor and Luke shouted, "Ready!"

Nathan counted down, "Three, two, *one!*"

The boards in the pile shifted slightly and Luke heaved, drawing Melinda out from beneath the pile in one smooth motion. The weight on Jack's shoulder became crushing as the beam responded to the shift.

Dev groaned and Jack shouted, "Get out Nathan. Now!"

Nathan scrambled out. "Clear!"

But Jack waited until they'd pulled Melinda clear of the roof, suspended by the outer supports like a collapsed soufflé, before he shrugged the beam off his shoulder and stood. The pavilion groaned ominously, so Jack grabbed hold of Dev's coat as Dev was grabbing on to Dean, and hustled them out from under what was left of the cover.

Releasing Dev, Jack ran to where Nathan and Connor were hunkered over the most important person in Jack's life. The realization that Melinda was indeed that made his breath hitch.

Her big brown eyes, looking darker than he'd ever seen them in her pale face, snagged on him and held. "Jack." She tried to lift an arm, but Nathan wouldn't let her, pausing as he unbuttoned her heavy barn jacket long enough to put her arm back down at her side. "You okay?" she asked, her voice reedy. It must hurt her to breathe.

Jack sunk down on his knees in the snow at her shoulder. This close he could see why her eyes appeared so dark—her pupils were blown wide. His chest grew tight again. She still might not be out of the woods yet. "Forget about me. How about you? In case you didn't notice, the sky just fell on your head."

She grinned, though it was clearly just for show. "Chicken Little was right." Then she flinched when Nathan pressed on her side. "How long was I out?"

"It seemed like an eternity, but I guess it couldn't have been more than a minute or two."

Her eyes grew shinny with moisture. "I'm sorry to have worried you, Jack."

Before he could reassure her with something that would have been a lie, Nathan sat back and blew out a huge breath. "Believe it or not, despite the fact that this particular sky was made up of huge hunks of wood, I think all that she has going here is an obvious concussion and maybe broken ribs.'' He spotted the backboard Kyle Mason had run to the medical clinic for. ''Ah, good,'' he said. ''Let's get her to the clinic and make sure. That X-ray machine I spent some of my lottery dough on sure is coming in handy.''

Telling himself his hands were shaking in relief, Jack helped the two doctors slide the backboard beneath her and fastened the Velcro strap that went over her chest.

Luke squatted next to him and softly asked, ''What happened here, Jack?''

Jack slowly shook his head in bewilderment. ''It just came down.''

''Do you think it was the wind?''

Looking up at the bare tree branches moving above them as the winter storm that had been predicted moved in, Jack said, ''A gust blew through and made the whole thing groan, but the wind wasn't blowing when it came down. And even when it was, I don't think it was blowing hard enough to bring the roof down. That pavilion has withstood winds a heck of a lot stronger than what's going on today.''

Luke nodded in agreement, his lips pressed into a grim line.

Jack looked back down at Melinda, who was following Connor's instructions as he fastened a thick, bright yellow, padded collar that was connected to the backboard around her neck. There was no blood, so her scalp hadn't been cut, but she would surely have a hell of a bump on the top of her head.

He met Luke's deep blue eyes again. "But there was a lot of snow built up on the roof. Isn't it supposed to be scraped off every now and again?"

Luke shifted his gaze to the collapsed pavilion. "Yeah, it is. But just like with the wind, I've seen more snow than that on the pavilion and it handled the load just fine. I'll have to get someone to look at it."

When they all stood, Dean stepped forward. "Here, Jack. Let me help carry her. You got whacked yourself." He pointed at Jack's head.

Jack started to reach up, unaware of anything except his fear for Melinda, but Dean's comment had caught Connor's attention, and with Melinda's neck collared and strapped to the board, he was free to reach over and stop Jack from touching his head.

Connor instructed, "Tilt your chin down." The same height as Jack, Connor had no trouble getting a good look at Jack's head. "Eh. Butterfly strip will probably be enough to close that. I'll take care of it as soon as we get Melinda checked out."

Jack finally noticed a warm trickle of wet at his hairline, and reached up to wipe the blood away under Dean's worried gaze. "It can't be much if that's all it's bleeding. I want to carry her." Hell, he'd rather gather her into his arms and rush her to the clinic himself, but Nathan and Connor were right to put her on a backboard.

Even though there were plenty of offers, he insisted on helping carry her along with Connor, Luke and Dev. She was so petite, two of them could have done it, but the object was to jostle her as little as possible, so four men were better. Nathan went ahead to prep.

Jack took the handhold near her shoulder so he could easily check her face for signs of pain, despite knowing she'd rather chew nails than let on how much she hurt. It wasn't until they were heading out that he noticed how many people were still milling around the park despite the fact that the weather had indeed turned. An icy wind blew steadily now, and along with it had come the snow-heavy cloud layer that lent a weird glow to the sky. There was no doubting that a blizzard was on its way.

But people hadn't gone home. And when they saw Melinda being carried out, everyone formed a sort of path so that they could give him and Melinda encouragement and well wishes as they went by. Wyla and Bobby were especially upset and vocal, wishing Melinda Godspeed like she was heading off on some sort of dangerous mission.

Jack's throat grew unmercifully tight. There was no way Melinda would be able to deny any longer that she had a place in this town.

His place.

With her accepted as the town vet, he'd be free to leave. Free to go someplace where he wouldn't know anyone, wouldn't care about them.

This close brush with losing her made him realize

how much he was risking by allowing himself to care for a woman this way again. He was so close to giving his heart to her, so close to loving her.

But he couldn't. He wouldn't survive losing the woman he loved again. Yeah, she hadn't died this time, but there were so many unexpected, uncontrollable things that could happen to her. The danger in their job was expected, part of the deal, and he trusted her skill enough to know that she'd minimize the danger by being careful. But there were so many things she didn't have control over, so many things he couldn't protect her from.

He couldn't risk loving and losing again. He wouldn't survive it.

He glanced down at her as they made their way into the Jester Medical Clinic. Carlie Goodwin, the clinic's receptionist, had rushed ahead with Nathan and held the door open for them. Melinda's eyes were closed and he could see the muscles straining in her jaw and neck as she clenched her teeth. She might be more seriously injured than Nathan had first thought.

Jack's heart spasmed painfully.

He had wanted to see how long this thing with Melinda would last, and now he knew. However deep his feelings for her might go—and judging by the searing pain in his heart, they went deep—he suspected they would last forever, but he couldn't allow this relationship to continue another day.

He couldn't keep her if he couldn't bear to lose her.

They carried her into the examination room Nathan had readied and placed her, backboard and all, on the bed. With the two doctors immediately going to work on her, Jack started to back out of the room.

"Jack?" Melinda called.

Connor stepped to the side so she could see him. Though the neck brace kept her from looking directly at him, he could see the worry on her face.

His guts twisting, he reassured her. "It's okay. I'll just be out here. I don't want to be in the way."

Connor said, "I'll come take care of that cut on your head in a second, Jack."

Jack waved him off. "You see to her. I can clean this up myself." He grabbed a couple packets of medicated gauze pads and left the room.

He'd planned on planting himself on one of the couches in the reception area, but everyone who'd helped him dig Melinda out was milling around there along with their wives, so he instead went into the other exam room and sat in a chair tucked next to the door. He cradled his head in his hands, finally noticing how much it was throbbing and bleeding, and closed his eyes, trying to shut out the all too familiar horror that came along with images of the roof collapsing onto Melinda. Now he had one more set of memories, one more set of circumstances—albeit with a better ending, but awful just the same—to haunt him here in Jester.

He should have already done what he'd planned for so long.

Leave.

FREEZING IN NOTHING but her off-white, wool boot socks and the open-backed gown they'd helped her into with discretely turned heads, Melinda tried her best to be a *patient* patient while Dr. Perkins and Dr. O'Rourke poked, prodded and X-rayed her. She already knew that besides having her bell rung pretty good, she was fine. But they were going over the X-rays of her ribs like a missed crack could cost her her life.

"Dr. Perkins, Dr. O'Rourke—"

"Nathan," Dr. Perkins insisted over his shoulder.

"Connor," Dr. O'Rourke said right after.

Their willingness to be familiar warmed her. She smiled. "Nathan, Connor, they aren't broken, are they?"

They both shook their heads.

As Connor reached to switch off the light board, Nathan said, "Amazingly, no. But they are badly bruised. I thought for sure that 4x6 I had to lift off you would have caused at least a crack, but you're a lot tougher than you look."

"You've clearly never seen me wrestle a steer down," she boasted to cover up her relief.

She didn't want anyone to treat her like she might break. The fact that she'd weathered having a roof drop on her without suffering any serious damage should go a long way to convince folks that her looks were deceiving. And that was important because after seeing the sort of response she could get from Jack when she dressed more feminine, she had no intentions of going back to her tomboy look ever again.

Still worried about the blood she'd seen smeared on Jack's forehead, she repeated the request she'd made several times already. "Would one of you then go and take care of Jack? He's the type to try to stitch his own head if it needs it."

Connor headed toward the door. "More likely he's sitting out there letting blood run down his face unnoticed because he's worrying about you."

The image of Jack bloody made her wince, which didn't help her own throbbing head. The pain reliever they'd given her hadn't kicked in yet. "Then have him come in when you're done with him, please. Unless, of course, I can get dressed and go out to him?" she asked hopefully.

Both of them looked at her like she was nuts.

Connor said, "I'll send him in." He then left the room.

Nathan came over to her, squinting as he looked into her eyes. "You're not going anywhere until I'm sure there are no complications stemming from your concussion."

"I was only out a minute or two."

"Which, as I'm sure you know, Dr. Woods, is a serious thing, for man or beast. So I'm going to heat you a blanket and get you settled for a while. I'll even let Jack climb up there to keep you company. Though I doubt your ribs will appreciate it." He winked and left the room.

Nathan's teasing went a long way to warming her

up. It made her feel like she belonged. How could
Jack not feel that way, too, surrounded by such wonderful people?

Jack came in after only a minute or two, instantly
filling the room, and Melinda, with his own brand of
heat. Her attention went straight to his head, and relief
washed through her to see it wasn't bandaged and the
blood had been cleaned away. But his eyes held a
look of pain that gave her a fresh jolt of worry. He
could have a more serious head injury than they'd
first suspected.

She reached out to him. "Let me see your head."

He waved away her concern, his gaze jumping to
the X-ray film hanging on the turned off light board
before coming back to her. "It's fine."

"Let me look anyway."

Relenting, he came to her side and bent down so
she could see the top of his head, his thick, light
brown hair darkened by dampness. He was bandaged,
after all, but only by a small, butterfly-shaped adhe-
sive strip that held closed the inch-long cut in his
scalp just above the hairline. Only a small amount
hair had been shaved so the butterfly would stick.

She reached to gently test the edges. "Did you put
it on?"

He straightened away from her touch, shaking his
head. "Connor."

"He's fast."

With a lift of his shoulder that didn't change his

solemn expression, he said, "I imagine being a pediatrician teaches you how to do what needs to be done quick."

Despite her concern for him, she smiled, imagining Jack ducking and bobbing like a kid who didn't want to be touched. "Did he give you a lollipop?"

Jack shook his head again, strangely unwilling to joke with her. He was also keeping his distance, which really surprised her. She'd fully expected to be crushed in his embrace by now. She needed it. She needed to be reassured that they had both survived a very frightening moment. She reached for him again but he moved away.

Melinda closed her hand around thin air and her worry grew until her heart pounded with it.

He eyed the backboard Nathan and Connor had left propped against the far wall after they'd determined her back wasn't injured, then he turned to brace his hands against the wall and dropped his head between his outstretched arms.

Her worry exploded into fear that left a metallic taste in the back of her throat. "Jack—?"

"Look, Melinda. What almost happened today has reminded me of…a few things." His voice had a strangled quality that she knew had nothing to do with the position he was in.

Barbed dread coiled around her heart and squeezed. She knew exactly what he meant.

Melinda's eyes welled with tears. "Oh, Jack. But everything turned out okay this time. I'm fine."

He pushed away from the wall and met her gaze. His green eyes were bright with anger. "But I'm not. And I'm never going to be if I open myself up to that sort of...of horror again. I can't do it, Melinda. I can't." He turned away from her and paced toward the door. "I can't risk caring about anyone so much again that the thought of losing them tears my guts out."

Melinda's own guts rebelled at his words and she feared she was about to be sick.

Jack put a hand to the doorknob, then looked back at her, the agony in his eyes hitting her harder than any roof ever could. "I plan to start packing up tomorrow. I should be finished and able to leave by the end of the week." He pulled in a shuddering breath. "I'm sorry, Melinda. So sorry. Goodbye."

## Chapter Fifteen

Melinda sagged in stunned disbelief, stupidly sitting there while Jack walked out of the exam room.

And out of her life.

Just like that, he was gone.

Anger flooded every pore like an unchecked fever.

All her life she had taken what was doled out to her, never complaining, never demanding she be given what she wanted, always hoping her hard work would earn the love and respect she needed. Well, no more. She was a grown woman who'd finally learned to speak up. Jack couldn't simply walk out of their relationship.

She wouldn't stand for it. There was too much at stake.

Melinda swung her legs off the exam table, gritting her teeth at the pain the motion fired through her ribs, and stood. Despite a reeling head, bruised ribs and an open-backed hospital gown, she wove her way to the door. She'd be damned if she let Jack walk away from her, from *them* like that. Without letting her have a chance to say a word. Of all the arrogant, *man* sort of things to do.

She faltered when she saw that the reception area was filled mostly with men, some of them looking a lot like the fuzzy twin of the guy next to them. But when she saw their attention was on the two Jacks heading out the clinic door, she frowned to clear her double vision, grabbed hold of the back of her gown and marched after him.

"Jack!" she called, but the door was already swinging shut behind him.

Connor and Nathan, who'd been talking to their wives, Shelly and Vickie, simultaneously scolded, "Melinda!"

Luke, who was closest, made a grab for her. "Melinda! You shouldn't be up."

She dodged his hand and staggered, bumping the side of her shin painfully against the coffee table covered with fanned-out issues of magazines like *Field and Stream* and *Cattleman's Weekly*. "Ouch. No, Luke. He's leaving. I have to stop him."

Luke got a hold of her then and steadied her, his big hand strong but gentle on her elbow. "Honey, I'm sure he just stepped out for—"

"No! He's leaving Jester. He's leaving *me*."

She watched the understanding dawn in Luke's clear blue eyes. "I understand, but let's get you—"

She pulled away from him. "There's no time." Before anybody else in the waiting room could say or do anything more, she hurried as best she could for the door.

Pressing an arm to her aching ribs while still gripping the gown closed with her other hand, she pushed the clinic door open with her shoulder and charged outside. A wave of dizziness rolled through her in time with the pounding of her head, but the cold hit her like a slap and helped her focus again.

"Jack!" she cried before she'd even looked around.

Then she stopped dead. What seemed like the entire population of Jester had turned to look at her with stunned expressions. People were milling around on the sidewalk and in the street in front of the clinic, clustered in groups of various sizes. Were they waiting in the cold for news of her? Did she matter enough for them to put aside their packing away of the Founders' Day celebration booths and decorations before the storm hit in full force?

Having no time to speculate about or process the possibility that she might have been accepted by the town, maybe even liked, she forced herself to search for Jack. Her gaze zeroed right in on his tall, broad form. He'd paused in what looked like the act of pushing through an undoubtedly interested group of people containing Stella, Irene, Gwen and her other regular, retiree boarder, Oggie Lewis. Jack looked as shocked and concerned as everyone else to see her standing outside.

Well, too bad.

Without a thought to the spectacle she was making of herself, she marched toward him, annoyed as hell that the cold wind blew up under her hospital gown and her socks wanted to stick to the dry snow. Judging by the amount already accumulated on the shoveled sidewalk, snow must have been falling since they'd taken her into the clinic. The blizzard the forecasters had predicted was clearly building up steam.

The frigid, stormy weather was a perfect match for her mood. "Damn it, Jack. You can't say what you just said and walk away. Not until I get a chance to say what *I* have to say."

His jaw set, Jack backtracked toward her, peeling his coat off. "For God's sake, Melinda," he growled and wrapped his coat around her shoulders. "You'll freeze out here."

She closed her eyes against the upswell of love for him as his heat and scent enveloped her.

He tugged the front of his coat closed. "Get inside before—"

"Not until you hear me out, Jack Hartman." She widened her stance and lifted her chin, doing her damnedest to let him know by looking at her how serious she was. His belief in her abilities and worth provided the courage she needed to make herself heard for the first time in her life.

She looked straight into his haunted green eyes and declared, "I love you." With a quick glance at the people around them, she lowered her voice a notch. "I mean I *really* love you."

His nostrils flared and he swallowed heavily.

"I'm not going to let you walk away from me, from us, that easily. You keep saying that you can't risk caring so much about anyone again, but I have news for you, Jack. It's too late. You already care for me. I know you do.'' Her voice hitched and she took a step closer to him, close enough she could feel the warmth radiating off him as his big body blocked the wind.

Her throat grew tight with the threat of tears, but she forced out, ''You could never hold me like you do, make me feel the things you do, if you didn't care.'' Her anger at him for putting them through this, for being so stubborn, built until her vision swam from tears, not dizziness. ''But you won't admit it, not even to yourself.''

She nodded her head toward the crowd listening with rapt attention. ''Just like you won't admit how much you care about them.''

Then an exclamation toward the back of the crowd near the park answered by worried sounding murmurs made her pause.

Melinda caught the words, ''The wolf,'' and ''Back away,'' just as the crowd parted and she could see what they were talking about.

With its head down in a wary stance near a clump of bushes not twenty feet away was the stray dog Jack had been after for weeks. Its boldness and feral look frightened those nearest to it, especially those holding corn dogs and other food still.

Sick to death of stubborn males, Melinda gave an unladylike snort, looked straight into the dog's dark eyes, pointed a finger at the ground next to her and commanded, ''Come!''

The dog's ears flattened, then it slunk toward her

after only the slightest hesitation, darting glances at those nearest as it went by. The closer it came to her, the lower it ducked, until it was practically on its belly by the time it reached her side and crouched in meek submission.

"Good dog," she praised the big, scruffy animal, then immediately leveled the same finger she'd pointed at the ground with at Jack. "Admit it, Jack. Admit how much you already care."

SHE LOVED HIM.

Jack rocked back on his heels, amazed not only by her declaration of love, but also by the simplicity of her solution for dealing with the stray dog. Yet it made perfect sense. The dog had clearly once been a pet, and most pets—even those not particularly loved—were taught to come when called.

She dropped her hand and shook her head in obvious frustration. "You keep saying that Jester isn't your town, that it had been Caroline's, but you are such a part of this place, I can't imagine it without you." She closed her eyes and pulled in a great, shuddering breath that must have hurt her ribs. "Just as I can't imagine my life without you."

A tear escaped from beneath her thick lashes and rolled down her pale cheek, opening a gash across his heart as it went.

She opened her eyes again and pleaded, "Why can't you let yourself be happy, Jack?"

It was a hell of a question.

Reeling, he reached up and cupped her chilled face

in his hand and wiped away the tear with his thumb. Could the cure for his pain be as simple as the solution for dealing with the stray dog? Could it be that perhaps like the dog, Jack had held his heart separate by choice, not circumstance?

He had indeed shared a kinship with the mutt. Jack had thought himself abandoned, lost to his surroundings and to the future he'd once thought he'd have thanks to a cruel, unexpected twist of fate. But he'd just been stubborn, unwilling to let himself be taken in by someone with heart enough to heal him, courage enough to care.

Melinda closed her eyes and nuzzled her face against his hand, then opened her beautiful brown eyes and looked right into his soul. "Loving is worth the risk, Jack. You, along with all your fellow millionaires," she stuck an arm out of his coat to gesture at those around them, "know exactly how well a risk can pay off."

A concurring murmur rippled through the crowd.

She grabbed hold of his shirtfront and tugged, the pain in her eyes tugging as effectively on his heart. "But you have to buy that ticket first. You have to take the risk. Please, Jack. Please take the risk."

Jack had rebelled against the notion of being connected with anything for so long it was hard to see past the habit to the logic in her words. Words that probably hadn't come easy to her, being a self-proclaimed woman of action. He thought back to her actions over the past few weeks. It was there. In the warm, deep safety of her brown eyes, in the coura-

geous—make that belligerent—set of her delicate jaw.

If he left town, would it make any difference?
Would he be any less worried about her or anyone
else here?

Would he love her any less?

And God, how he loved her.

He looked around to the concerned faces of the
people gathered in front of the clinic, people who had
been his family both before and especially after he'd
lost Caroline. He'd tried to hold his heart separate
after the car accident, cutting himself off from his
own parents and brother by keeping only minimal
contact. But he hadn't been able to do that with those
here in Jester.

Jack realized in a bolt of clarity that he couldn't
run from love any more than he could hide how much
Melinda and the whole town had come to mean to
him.

Melinda's teeth started to chatter, jarring him with
the reminder that her legs were bare and she had nothing on her feet but socks. Hell, she shouldn't be standing, let alone outside in this weather. He bent and
reached for the backs of her legs, intent on carrying
her inside.

She dodged away from him. "No. Not until you
answer me."

He straightened and crossed his arms over his
chest, his heart about ready to explode with love for
her. "Answer you? I think you need to answer me,
first."

"About what?" she demanded.

"Two things. First, do you intend to keep the dog?" He inclined his head at the animal who looked as if he meant to stay at her side forever.

She raised her chin still higher. "Of course I do. I even know what I'm going to name him already."

Jack raised a brow, loving her spirit and generous heart. "Oh?"

"I think Buck is the perfect name."

A ripple of subdued laughter went through the crowd.

Jack fought a grin as his pride in her and his appreciation for her humor swelled out of control. "All right." He looked deep into her dark chocolate eyes and drew the determination he needed from her. "Second, I want to know if you'll agree to do the one thing that will make me stay."

She stilled, without so much as a shiver. "What's that?"

He sucked in a lung full of bracing cold air. "Marry me."

Melinda's eyes went wide and her pretty mouth formed a small *O*, then her look turned wary.

Jack thought of all the times she'd been hurt by the men in her life, all the reasons she had not to trust him. He wanted to wrap her up in his arms and shelter her from that kind of pain for the rest of her life.

She narrowed her eyes at him. "Why?" Clearly she wouldn't allow herself to trust until she heard him say the words.

He intended to spend a lifetime not only saying

what she needed to hear, but showing her what was in his heart, also.

He lifted a hand and brushed the backs of his knuckles along the downy softness of her cheek. Her skin was warm despite the frigid air. She'd somehow managed to bring enough warmth back into his life to completely thaw the frost that had encased his heart for so long. "Because I love you and I want to buy you that ring you thought up with the big old diamond and two emeralds."

She squealed and launched herself at him. She gripped his neck so tight he worried about her ribs. "Yes, Jack. Oh, yes yes yes *yes!*"

A whoop went up from those around them.

In his ear she whispered, "I'll marry you Jack, with or without the big bucks."

\*    \*    \*    \*    \*

*Come back next month
for another installment of*
MILLIONAIRE, MONTANA.
*Don't miss*
*SURPRISE INHERITANCE*
*by Charlotte Douglas.*

*Available March 2003, only from Harlequin
American Romance.*

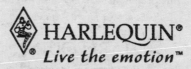

# From Regency Ballrooms to Medieval Castles, fall in love with these stirring tales from Harlequin Historicals

## On sale March 2003

### THE SILVER LORD by Miranda Jarrett

Don't miss the first of **The Lordly Claremonts** trilogy! Despite their being on opposite sides of the law, a spinster with a secret smuggling habit can't resist a handsome navy captain!

### FALCON'S DESIRE by Denise Lynn

A woman bent on revenge holds captive the man accused of killing her intended—and discovers a love beyond her wildest dreams!

## On sale April 2003

### LADY ALLERTON'S WAGER by Nicola Cornick

A woman masquerading as a cyprian challenges a dashing earl to a wager—with the stake being an island he owns against her favors!

### HIGHLAND SWORD by Ruth Langan

Be sure to read this first installment in the **Mystical Highlands** series about three sisters and the handsome Highlanders they bewitch!

**Harlequin Historicals®**
Historical Romantic Adventure!

# SAVOR THE BREATHTAKING ROMANCES
# AND THRILLING ADVENTURES
# OF THE OLD WEST
# WITH HARLEQUIN HISTORICALS

## On sale March 2003

### TEMPTING A TEXAN by Carolyn Davidson

A wealthy Texas businessman is ambitious, demanding
and in no rush to get to the altar. But when a beautiful
woman arrives with a child she claims is his niece,
he must decide between wealth and love....

### THE ANGEL OF DEVIL'S CAMP by Lynna Banning

When a Southern belle goes to Oregon to start a new
life, the last thing she expects is to have her heart
captured by a stubborn Yankee!

## On sale April 2003

### McKINNON'S BRIDE by Sharon Harlow

While traveling with her children, a young widow falls
in love with the kind rancher who opens his home and
his heart to her family....

### ADAM'S PROMISE by Julianne MacLean

A ruggedly handsome Canadian finds unexpected love
when his fiancée arrives and he discovers she's not the
woman he thought he was marrying!

**Harlequin Historicals®**
Historical Romantic Adventure!

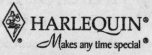

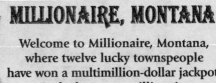
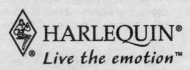